Books by Hortense Calisher

The Railway Police

and

The Last Trolley Ride

HORTENSE CALISHER

The Railway Police
and
The Last Trolley Ride

Little, Brown and Company · Boston · Toronto

LIBRARY OF CONGRESS CATALOG CARD NO. 66–16561

FIRST EDITION

*Published simultaneously in Canada
by Little, Brown & Company (Canada) Limited*

PRINTED IN THE UNITED STATES OF AMERICA

For
Katherine Squire
and
George Mitchell

The Railway Police

THIS time yesterday morning, I was sitting in one of the coaches of the Mayflower, the early New York to Boston train, on my way to take part in a panel at the monthly meeting of the Interagency Council of Supervisors, a professional organization to which I belong. Inside me, that tender, inverse psyche we all carry within us was as usual at once violently proud of its outer costume and at the same time making mock of it: silk suit sharp-creased for speechmaking, all underwear appropriate to legcrossing on platform, handbag by X, shoes by Y — all a perfect beige armor stopping just short of the creature-skin that no Florida can tan, inside which the little lady sits, quiet and not always sad, in her altogether, of that tint so much too nacreously fair.

And a hat — I am always extra careful about the hat. A person who wears a wig has to be. In bygone days — think of it, only a year or so ago — a person who had to wear a wig was still special, and buying a hat was for her, one might say, an affair of the double incognito, the purchase of a crown to place upon the crown that no one must know she already wore. Particularly if at the bottom of it all, beneath hat, wig, armor and skin, there was still caged but not coffined, ready to run if not rampant, the laughing tomboy of thirteen, putative cabinboy of fifteen, dockside loafer, bankrobber's mascot and Fagin's modern wonderboy in blue jeans and plimsolls with the tips of his fingers emeried; all shapes and types of tramp-Raffles riding the rods under the scurrying cries of the railway police — confidence makers and takers thumbing their young stowaway noses from soup kitchens to the sub-basements of all the Statler-Hiltons, freeloading and riding all the flowery, Bowery subcircuses of the world. All of them wearing caps, none of them grown past twenty, and none quite yet bald. My present profession makes it possible for me to observe quite selflessly that my imagination only took up its orthodox womanhood at the moment when the head which caged it had lost its last trace of hair.

The train was just getting into Providence, Rhode Island, due at 10:52, and on time. I know every curve and tockety of the Shore Line, having done all my later studies in Boston, with training trips from there to New York City, that even richer source for our stock-in-trade. It was wise of me to come East after Cooksley Normal; though the wig I bought on the way, in Chicago's Loop, was not very good, it

[4]

was better than the wrap-around turbans I had been wearing. And Boston, as everyone knows, is tops in social work — there being, further, no mystery as to why this profession should be mine. Even back in Cooksley, I had no trouble with psychological essences and timbres — after all, we had the same magazines as the rest of the country — and my education merely thrust me deeper back upon my own meanings.

For, very early during my practice days "in the field," as the pretty word for it goes in the profession, I knew that, via my work, the sores and seams of my own romanticism were being kept in sight for me at the very time I needed this — for who can say to what imaginations a bald beauty (I am otherwise comely) might not at any time revert? This way, all the while I toured the underworld I loved, a dainty Dante in her own laurel wreath, I was being kept a lady, or being made into one. None of my supervisors then or now (for all who work with the poor must have comptrollers who help keep our heads clear and well-hatted) has ever had to remind me that my work was sublimating me, though they mayn't have known in quite what terms.

And it is natural, therefore, that I have risen in it, though still well under thirty-nine. For I have never wholly deserted the field for deskwork, as most do as soon as possible, though I deserve no credit for having now and then a fierce need to carry slops and mealtickets to the midnight alleys, or to slog the mean streets in search of the company of those tucked jolly under the viaduct, around the fire made after the cop has made his last round, there to watch how, at dawn, the waterbugs streak like lizards from the Chinese restaurant, and at any hour men stride like catamounts, from plain doors.

There's not much danger; this is the neighborhood of my "case-load," where my hat, with its flowers of charity wired by law, probably affrights them, and I am more than likely to end up for a glass of tea with some old client, my one revolutionary gesture to sit, in all my niceties, on the bedbug couch she warns me away from, "Dun sit, dolling, Om afraid fom de boggles, dun sit dere."

And I know very well that this is still the world of the poor who live in houses, not vagabondage, just as I know that the poor, at least in cities, are not maypole dancers, their bread not oaten but paper. But their world is still a netherworld ringing from beneath the rich pavements they walk on just as I do. Even the poor in houses are only one step away from the criminal, for they have so much to hide that they can never do it quite honestly. Clean as they might be, they are still gamy, haunted and ridden by barmecide illusion, and I fancied I had almost a right to their underworld by way of my little specialty; I could walk their underside a little way with them, wearing my wig.

[6]

The train ran slowly to a stop; the conductor calling out "Providence!" had already been through the train, opening doors. Fresh gushes of air came from them, uniting with the warm, sunny velvet coming in on me from the broad window, outside which houses, running like sixty the minute before, settled into the dull station-scene brilliant in the morning sun, ultimate stillness. The pause at Providence is approximately two minutes, forty seconds, when the train is running on schedule. I was sitting on the double seat just back of the washrooms, the one on the platform side, facing the door. Waiting to get off, there was the usual crowd, trim salesmen with their noses elongated by money-sniffing (the real money flies the air, of course), aunties in hats-on-a-visit, a ruck of the indefinable, middling personages who do crowd-service, starred with the one sweatered girl who is always going down the aisle, jiggle-breasted, to the Women's. The air, once past the train-smell, came in pure and lively, the fresh vanilla perspiration of spring; it was March twenty-first, one day into spring.

And it was just then that I saw the young man hovering on the step, ready to jump off ahead of them all. He must just have come out of the washroom. I saw him from the inside of the coach, and only the back of him. He was tall, had a good head under a good crop of hair, and was dressed in a suit of which trousers even matched jacket; it needed a second glance to see, doubletake, that, yes, from top to toe, though I couldn't see his shoes, he was one fatal thread away from the tidy civilization of the train. The head had been to the barber, but not the last time, the suit was tired from making do, and as he leaned, head bent, hands slouched in pockets, shoulder taking bearings from the wall the way a zoo animal does, I caught, though I was yards away, the whole posture and lion-soil of him — a vagrant, in unmistakable aquiline.

He must have been readying himself to make a running jump for it. For almost in that same moment, I saw through the window the bright, gold-rimmed bumpkin face and blue uniform of the railway police, who put out arms to receive him, and behind in the coach, the conductor's cap, his pale face blotted in the crowd. They handed him over, uniform to uniform. He must have been in the washroom, ticketless. And if he had only permitted himself a hat perhaps or the cheapest cardboard dispatch case, just one patch of greasepaint to keep him on the right side of the line, he might have made it. Perhaps they telegraphed ahead from New London or wherever he had boarded; though it might seem a lot of trouble for just a ticket, it is by taking just such infinite pains that the upper parallel keeps itself from meeting the lower.

For through the window, I saw him led off, and there was that about him which made me sure the offense was no worse than this; he was walking straight and unalcoholic, not with the tension of the really hunted, with the experienced resignation of one who knew himself to be no more than a matter for the railway police. Head still a little bent, hands out of his pockets now and hanging down, he let himself be led along by this round pattycake of a man, winded too, from whom he could have darted like a whippet from its starter. I hadn't had a look at his shoes, of course, and he may have been too hungry. But I caught the line of his jaw and cheeks, good ones too, but just a hairsbreadth, again just a hairsbreadth too unshaven, and something in me trolled out to him, "Oh la-la, that did it. You might still have made it — if you had shaved."

In retrospect, I have the feeling he knew that as well as I did. Two days more of that beard, and he could have been a student growing one, even with that suit on him perhaps, but not — no never — not ticketless too. It takes keeping up, any posture of what you are not, takes a sense of fitness to the point of fashion, and the vagrant won't bother with that sort of thing, not for that purpose, he's too honest for it, or else he wants to be spotted; maybe it's his very function in life to wander about thus exposed, so that others may find their signals in him. They led him toward the steps of a small, official-looking hut a short distance across the station yard, and just then it happened. One of his coattails flipped up, not jaunty,

not especially sad either, it may even have been the
wind that did it, not his hand, and I saw a piece of
white shirt, fairly clean, and a belt going round a
human axis. All I had caught was a two-minute-and-
forty-second glimpse of his simple, hopeful domestic
arrangements. And that was all I needed. I never
even saw him go up the steps.

I took action at once — as is usually said of themselves by persons who have been hearkening for
twenty years. Such action, boiled up out of meditation, is often absurd unless it goes straight to the
heart of the matter, and I did not do that at once — I
was not quite able. To unprepare oneself for such a
journey is not easy, particularly when it is one that
may occupy the rest of your life. I told myself — tim-
idly, I agree — that my proper embarkation would
be from that place where so much of the rest of me
was, from all that other paraphernalia by which we
extend our pet fantasies of ourselves without ever
risking the depots of travel — from home.

Inside the washroom, meanwhile, I removed gloves,
stockings and girdle, and thrust them under the sink,
into the receptacle for used paper towels — a ridicu-
lously minor performance to be sure, but in the light
of the whole, it doesn't matter now. As for baggage,
it has always been my grief that I could never travel
as executively light as even the ticket-world now can.
I had, to be sure, my little modern portfolio of
articles that thimbled or stretched or reversed them-

selves, of paquettes that exploded for one use, then melted away — but I also had my wig-box, the over-night one. Made for me, like the larger ones, by a theatrical supply house, it had just room enough for the wig I made use of to sleep in — ah, the comfort of mind, when I learned to do that! — plus a fresh one for morning, and of course it didn't look like what it was.

Nowadays, markedly within this past, disturbing year, wig-boxes have become all too common; though they still keep mostly to the airlanes and the parlor cars, I look for them in the coaches and even the buses by the year's end — if I myself am able to risk such vehicles at that time. Meanwhile, peeping into mine, I quickly disposed of the portfolio down the slot where the girdle had gone, then tried the sealed window, in vain. The kit itself would have to be abandoned either here or on the luggage-racks outside. Gazing into it, down at the wooden wig-blocks on which my other two rested, I concluded that the latter's destiny would have to be linked with that of their eighteen sisters, this number being an accident of the calendar, seven for the week, plus certain other considerations. In place of these two, I now left my hat, for the Easter joy of some train-man's wife in Canarsie or Brookline. Then, shoulder-ing the kit, I looked at my image in the mirror.

"No," I finally said to it. "Not down an aisle. No drama." The true vagrant, honor-bright refuser of houses, clothing, income and other disguises, appears as my young man of the coattails had appeared to me, unaware of the comment he makes by existing. I could never be that unsophisticate — or perhaps, only after years of the discipline, by the time I had come to be an old abbess of the byways, worn back into simplicity at last after a misspent youth in the world. My present object must be to conduct myself, though within the framework, with all possible reserve — for there is always the question of sanity raised in re those who give up the things of this world. (And today, I already yearn to do it with — yes, it must be said — with beauty. But yesterday, I hadn't come that far.)

Smiling wryly, I said to myself, "Take it easy. Give yourself a headstart."

It's a thing of mine to make puns like that to myself, which no one else notices, nothing but a compensatory psychological adjustment, quite harmless and quite natural — and one which has helped until todate to keep me well short of the adjustment that is the most natural of all. But that was yesterday. When I reopened the door of the washroom, less than fifteen minutes had passed. I was back in my seat, with all plans figured out except for the final contingency ("case closed" it is sometimes called, in the profession) by the time we rolled into the stop for suburban Boston: Route 128.

I used to know the 128 stop very well. All one

summer, a man who, as the saying goes, was once
very important to me, used to meet me there with a
car. Cars free people; in summer particularly, they
are the vagabondage of the ticketed world. And no
matter what season of the year I pass that station, I
breathe in again the hot organdy smell of my own
sleeveless dresses, of sour-wine picnics where the
wine couldn't wait any more than we could, and of
meadow-love. Outdoor love is easiest for those who
must beware the midnight-rumpling hand. Inside the
waiting room, where I had to sit when he was late
or it was rainy, the majestically coifed, redheaded
stationmistress used to sit eternally in her little box-
office, talking now and then in camaraderie with the
round-faced policeman whose detail was 128. As far
as I could see, he never did anything but point out
the phone booth to people who had missed connections, or alert the crowd on the platform to the
warning bell rung for an oncoming engine — as far
as I could see then. After that summer was over,
I more than once dreamt of the stationmistress with
her masses of hair, not a wig but dyed, and not the
plain dark red, neither bronze nor carroty, of the
color which, until I was twelve, had been mine.

"One-twenty-eight," the conductor called now,
jumping off; it's a very short stop. I had no intentions
of getting off there, now or ever again, but as always,
I leaned to look. Usually I saw the policeman, the
same one, and once, in a snowy winter, I had seen

the woman shoveling — and seeing them was always
like a momentary return to a village where people
are so little on the move that one can see clearly how
all the life-stories have worked out, including one's
own. I didn't see her now, but I saw the policeman,
same old pieface in dark blue. They must rear a race
of them from the cradle, I thought, nanny-faces all,
puzzled, even kindly, with waists too big for wearing
holsters. For though this one wore no gold-rims, in
every respect there was no doubt otherwise. He was
a ringer for the one in Providence. Or else his
brother. And suddenly my ungloved hands sought to
hide themselves, my nude shins rubbed nervously
together, and I shrank away from the window, a
warning ringing inside me. "Chickie!" it said. "Watch
out for the railroad dicks!"

At first I was disturbed by this menial response,
one so much lacking the insouciance I had expected,
but then reminded myself that with my clothes still
elegant, my purse stuffed, such a halfway state of
mind was at least sensitive; I had after all scarcely
touched upon, much less completed, my full conver-
sion. The minute I thought of this latter, the
fluttering pulse in my throat was silenced, and an
enormous but active peace settled on me; only dwell
on the crowning event that was coming toward me,
and all the smaller stratagems flew to hand. After
that everything went swimmingly.

I got off at South Station, filled out a telegraph

form "Unavoidably detained," changed the latter to "prevented," and grabbed a cab to Logan Airport, in time to board a shuttle plane which would even get me back to New York before bank-closing. Though incomes in my line are never impressive, my mixed family inheritance did include money, not enough, alas, to have allowed me that comfortable eccentricity which might have put me to rights in the very beginning, but there is no doubt that in a modest way I am a woman of property. From now on, the problem would be how to disencumber myself, down to the bone as it were, without incurring the verdict of either sainthood or insanity. I had no wish to decamp altogether, like those irresponsibles who dissolved themselves in a puddle of clothes left on the beach at Villefranche, or from an ownerless car on the Golden Gate Bridge. Any one of these eventualities would make me a mystery, not, as I faintly hoped, a statement. I regret that there's also no doubt that I suffer from a certain ambition, akin perhaps to that of women just before they got the vote — a kind of suffragette swelling, part yearning and part vengeful, of the chest cavity and maybe even the heart. I am well aware that the true vagrant never even knows the nature of what he cherishes, in his case his right to be out of the organized world. Later on, I hope in my own way to achieve that brahma; I see myself holding up my naked head without knowing that I am doing it. Right now, however, though I deplore it, I want all the civil rights in my category.

And so it's not surprising that the minute I got on the plane I started mulling what else I could take off, substitute gestures to placate that fire in me raging toward the ultimate one. Inside the washroom again, the only disposal unit that modern transportation allows us, I made friends again with my image. I was wearing my platform wig, its clubwoman curls now blown by airport and emotional currents into a bad semblance of one at home marked in my mental roster as Careful Disarray, but verging more on the brown than the blonde. (It is discreetly known at the office that I dye my hair myself, not always accurately.)

I regarded it, but was glad to feel full and strong in me the power to delay — "No, not yet. No travesty."

As for statutory nudity, it had no charms for me at this point, indeed the reverse; exhibitionism was at all costs to be avoided. Teeth were excellent *and* personal, eyes never in need of glasses — the clear green eyes born to lucky people of my complexion.

Just then the stewardess knocked, and I watched my hands seek themselves.

"Quite all right!" I managed to say — this time, God save us, with some proper daring in it, and a minute later I was taking off my rings.

To my left there was a ventilator, whose exhaust slot must somewhere reach the outer air. The shuttles don't fly very high, not nearly so high as the pan-orient jets on which I suppose I started my hunt for brahma in the first place. Crouched there, in my palm the little hoard to which I had added lapel-pin and pearls, I waited until we were well away from water, over a tiny settlement where I might predict, if not see, spire and gardens, a railway station too perhaps; then with a smile, imagining on whom that shower of peculiar manna, sent them down.

Back in my seat again, I had certain canny misgivings, the tiresome ones of a woman with too many heads. How small did a diamond have to be not to burst its facets from such a height, how light a pearl, not to smash its baroque? I had retained my watch, and I had an hour to consider the lost rings of all those who had loved me, plus that most durable of all, the invisible wedding-band I had never let myself receive.

What of love, then, for such a woman, for any — for anybody, what of love?

My mother's mother's snakeband ring with emerald eye and my father's father's onyx seal I had worn joined on one finger, cabalistic bow to that minor hitch in the vortex of heredity which had caused me. Dear supervisors all, should they at the agency ever know the circumstances (and I might in time send

[17]

them the case-record) — I could hear the descant that would follow, in the ballet of headshakes that always formalizes psychological gossip.

. . . (Would it have been better if the departed's trauma had come to her through some normal community way such as radiation sickness, instead of having been visited upon her via the single, traumatic shock of birth? . . . What hopes could be held for a girl whose own sibling would one day ask her, eighteen years to her sixteen: "Haven't *you* begun to . . . lose any of it . . . all over, yet?" . . . And who then would add in a whisper, turning away a face already shorn of brow and lash, a head already ennobled to its own bone — "What about . . . *down there?*") . . .

Ah, we had our ribald humors, my brother and I, but that day wasn't one of them, not when I had to answer him — for I was never to be as bad a case as he, and still have, though so faintly auburn, eyelashes — when I had to answer him . . . "No." And on the record, I had a word of advice for them, my friends at the agency. Don't be so quick to asperse birth, the plain fact of our beginnings. And don't believe anything but the facts:

Subject (who is I) *and sibling born to elderly well-to-do emigré parents.* Perhaps we were menopausal babies conceived after danger of such was deemed

[18]

over, since both my parents, as distant cousins from same ancestral town, were well aware of hereditary traces.

Both deceased during infancy of children, who were brought up under amiable legal guardianship, to best U.S. standards of oranges, lambchops, orthidonture and quarterly anti-pronation shoe-fittings.

From extant pics of parents aetat 35, my father's hairline may have been retouched, my mother's even more susceptible to illusion.

Hereditary condition well documented in European medical annals (though not endemic there) via easier observation in small, genealogically related loci, such as the German, North Sea town where my grandparents still reside.

May or may not be Mendelian recessive, thought by some to be albino-related, no official name. (Not alopecia areata, which is temporary.)

Males invariably lose facial as well as scalp-hair, fem. data less procurable though subject recalls, from youthful visit to grandparents, family portraits ranging back to the medieval, in which coif-line was shown almost as far back behind ears as a bridle.

Classically appears at onset of puberty, when natal hair of a characteristically silky dark-red gives way to carroty coarse growth which in turn disappears partially or in toto, usually by time of patient's majority. N.B. from subject: We were classical.

And in fancy I could read, over their shoulders,

my evaluation (after group study of further history up to March 21st):

Subject, aided by economic status and first-class appliances, has made excellent progress in resolving toward conventional norms the original handicap of birth. Irredentist impulses not to be taken too seriously. As cosmetic use of wigs gains community-wise, subject's sense of unity with the general population will increase. Subject's quasi-humorous diagnosis of her sublimation to be taken as a real testimonial to our profession, fine objectivity from one of the solidest gals in the office.

And down in the corner of our biannual personality sheet I could even read a handwritten scrawl from my immediate supervisor: *Mildly bizarre thoughts a good sign of nonrigidity. Do I detect a sign that my quiet one may be getting espoused? Hats off!*

With all the abstract sociological kindness going about the world, it's hard to get a true story listened to on the level, even by oneself. What could I say, for instance, of my brother, become that perennial movie star whose trademark is hairlessness (in his case not however like old Von Stroheim, a villain, or a horror man like Peter Lorre, but cast as a straight romantic hero). Rumor has it that he is forbidden by contract to show so much as a single hair, some saying that he complies only by means of terrifying sessions of electrolysis, others that he keeps a young valet-of-the-tweezers ever by his side. When first out in the world, we used to envy one another, I him for his public baldness, he me for my disguise. Now we no longer saw each other, having usefully agreed, like enemies in entente, that we no longer had anything in common. Like many ties of love, ours was too painful to eat dinner with.

And so — I looked at my watch — I was back to love again, only twenty minutes out of Logan. And I had two more rings to dispose of in memory.

On the fourth finger of my right hand, where unmarried women often wear a parental diamond or an engagement ring that hasn't worked out, I had worn, until yesterday, a small blue-white Tiffany in platinum, of the size given virgins by young men on modest budgets, as indeed it had been, by the one all hands would have said I should have married, the medical student, childhood friend and sole remaining witness of all my real changes, who had followed me East — and who had declined to make good his promise of marriage if I aborted the child he had already engendered.

"We could adopt some," I said.

"No," he replied, "I want our own first, if you don't mind. I'm going to become a gynecologist."

And so he has done, fat as a woodchuck too, and full of Christmas cards. But he was thin then, and staunch, and what he said sounded unanswerable. I wanted to answer it, at the time still believing that the apogee of life would be to have one secret witness forever at my side.

"But *I* mind!" I said. "I should mind forever. For *them*." He shrugged, and I caught him looking with distaste at the wig I had just bought — the first one.

"Children can learn to be bald," he said.

I was wounded beyond reason by this coldness.

"Already we differ," I said. "Not mine."

I handed him his ring back, strange gesture across the child I still carried (and stranger miscalculation?) for I understood his intent now — to bring me with it, out into the open.

"Keep the ring at least," he said. "Keep it until you marry. Until you do, girl with your looks and plans might find it useful. You can always tell them I died in a war."

Though I never did, it's true that both colleagues and lovers have sometimes murmured to me that one should not cling to the past, so perhaps his ring had been part agent of what he would never have done himself — helped me to hide the present that clung to *me*.

When I tried again to return the ring, he grasped me, shook me, even repeated his cold remark.

"Ours could learn!" he added, shouting. He stood there, hirsute and flawless, as his cards show him yet, the rufous glints all over the backs of his hands, not a spot of baldness in him anywhere, far as I could see, either of the body or the heart. And he could say that to me. It was a beautiful declaration, and I have never yet had another like it. But I knew at that moment why I was right to refuse him. To be acceptable, such declarations must come to the bald — from the bald.

And so we arrive at the man from 128, if not for long.

In the meantime, I had had my further experiences in the dark, not many, and never with any candidate to whom I could see myself making any such avowal — despite which I sometimes found myself in serious need to repress the more ordinary part of my inheritance: almost any woman's urge to avow. So I gave up such doings, and returned to the midnight safety of my old alleyways, to slouching in cool raincoats at the hot bedsides of their sick, sitting up at the wakes of their hardy sorrows, or kicking up the orange dawn in the circle of such derelicts as were too far gone to wonder at the presence of a lady at that fire. Weekends I spent emotion thriftily in the colorful melancholia of the museums and the Sunday exhibitions, quietly enjoying the arts and gems that were the property of the nation.

For this conduct, the gods duly corrected my position in life as they saw fit, from the rear. I received a salary increase, my largest block of securities held a stock-split, and there fell due a trust fund for which I had done nothing but get older. In one of the galleries I was in the habit of visiting, there was a small picture, not for sale, a Picasso of a certain period of his so in sympathy with my life that when I stood in front of it my flesh crept toward it as if it were my ikon. I went to see it again, the money shining in my head, making my brain all one large emerald. And there I met him, or rather, his rich voice, coming round a plush, impressionist corner. I fell in love with what he was saying before I saw him.

It was one of the tender, warm April after-noons that climb like vines from the most ruined steppes of a metropolis; rays of Central Park were falling all over the city and amoretti flew the wind. Any woman with verve in her veins was carrying her beauty like a cup. From my apartment, modestly high in Tudor City, I had seen that, and I was wearing my mother's tourmalines, which are of a peculiar burnt color, like cream glazed by the cook's salamander, plus a silk shift, sweater and sandals of the same, all designed to cast their tans against a skin that could not tan, and at the last minute I had put on the wig that was my bravest, most costly, favor-ite, if I could be said to have favorites among them, and unworn since I had last dined with my brother — a wig that was as flat to the face as a wig dares to be, and of a plain dark red. It was a wig that would not suffer a hat, nor would I have asked it to, but had anchored it instead with the best of many long-tried substances, pins not being possible for me. (If I mention these frail beauties, sands of makeshift, it is to remind myself, via all I have abjured, of the sterner exquisite I am to become.)

Anyway, as always happens in these fateful meetings, I got there just in time and properly rigged for it, in time to hear him say to the dealer, in a voice rich enough to buy Picassos, which is what he was there for: "Ah, come on, Knoller, you have me over the barrel, if you'll part with it. Kept thinking of it all the time I was away. Most of all in Bangkok. Monks with shaved heads, widows too, often just the common people. Modern Giacometti, sculpture without curls. I tell you, you've never seen the glory of the unadorned human head before. Of course, set against all that incredible gilt temple-patchwork, maybe any passing human skull is a Buddha. And it may be the Asiatic head only or the African — or that you get accustomed to seeing it in both sexes. I certainly never think of it in Rome."

There was a muffled remark from the dealer, and another rich, amused reply. "No, I guess the Western head can't compete, not even the ones bared by nature." And then, "Well, Knoller? What do you say?"

He was standing, as I knew he must be, in front of my picture.

"Here's your rival," Knoller said to him.

I saw the eyes change, lit as if passed over by the salamander. He smiled at me, a tall, powerfully set man not yet fifty and only partially tonsured by time,

[25]

lean cheeks with a center vertical like a knifed dimple, the strong nostrils that were said to go with large organs of generation, a mouth with a firm ripple. In the end, it was only the dealer who held out.

An affair begun in that season, with the trees just on the point of flower, seems to keep pace with them, with the apple, the cherry and the peach. There was much that was invisible on both sides. His household, which I saw no point in entering, was being supervised for him by his French mother-in-law: I saw the dead wife's picture, her gamine haircut and tiny phiz, like a stableboy in hornrims, and the two children, all three astride horses and wearing seedy clothes that did no justice to their mounts. They could live the preciously simple life that such money can, the kind that if one can forget what manages it at the top and sustains it from below, can sometimes even have a haystack whiff of the vagrant — and can make love in its own meadows. I was not seduced by its attractions, merely by him. When it rained, we stayed in the carriage-house, a mile from the main drive. I never stayed overnight, being always on the way to Boston, and when he came to the city we met, afternoons only, in the flat of one of his friends.

It was outdoors that I was most daring, though the wig I wore was never again the red one. I got him to tell me, over and over, about the monks in Bangkok, and the widows. His own hairline, receded to well back of the crown and worn in a rough tuft there, I persuaded him to have cropped close by the barber, as many men do. His cranial bump was large, and the effect not very fine, but in certain half-lights, country dusks, I thought I could feel a kinship, surely in my case not perverse. He began even to think of publishing, under the auspices of the museum he served without fee as curator, a monograph on the nude head in ancient entablature (and life, of course); there was even, he said, a question of such as having existed beneath the elaborate Etruscan . . .

"Ah well," he said, breaking off and looking down at me fondly, "there's always some question or other about the Etruscans. And why bother your pretty head — " Like any man, he thought that I was developing a flattering interest in his interests, and I, trembling on the verge of delight, thought that he — God help us, and all pairs of lovers. And, very gently indeed, the gods corrected us, from the rear.

I raised myself on elbow, in the lush grasses on which the first pinched windfalls were lying. "I'll shave my head for you!" I said. "I'll — " Pride shook me for what I could show him, for what I could at last bare to that perceptive eye. "Then you can see what a *Western* head . . . I mean it."

His smile showed no incredulity at the depth of my devotion. Then he enfolded me. There flashed before me a sudden picture of the stripling wife, of those buried tastes which men, and women too, were

[27]

said to have without knowing, but I blotted it out, blaming my over-educated inner eye. Yet I knew that for both of us it was the moment of the not impossible lover — or the moment just before.

"No," he said afterwards. "I'll be the bald one. That's still a man's job." He reached for me again. "Silly curls. I like them." He rumpled them, paterfamilias.

I gazed up at him from my end-of-summer headpiece, so artfully stained with sun-and-saltwater, and made myself remember, as I had been taught, that even in the love-duets of clods, the roles to be played are said to be endless. And then he asked to marry me. And then I invited him home.

He came down the next week, the first of my vacation, and, if we wished it to be, of our honeymoon. Despite this, I had done no extra shopping, having told myself that all honeymoons were — or should be — a mere matter of unveiling. I had asked him to meet me at a downtown theatre-club where an African singer he had never heard was appearing, and before I left my rooms I sat for a moment in their center, shivering in my decolletage, though it was warm September.

The apartment was no nondescript; I had done better than that. It was the proper guise for a professional woman of some means and culture, created for the pleased surveillance of my colleagues, with here and there a few endearing — and safe —

touches of family. Before I left, I locked the wig closet which had been put in off the dressing room, feeling as always, as I did so, that in a way I enclosed a seraglio of my selves.

They are very human-looking: wigblocks. At least, mine were. And I had no intention of shocking my dear love by the sudden grotesque of such a lineup, or of in any way taking out on him whatever of the harsher facts had been dealt me. No, I only meant to break to him, by stages, what I already thought he suspected and was waiting for — as courtiers in the old tales waited, in the dark of the robing room or the bedhangings, for the queen's maid to become the queen.

As I passed a bookshelf, I took up a little Parian bust, of some bewigged English jurist, picked up not long before in a junkshop, only because, aside from its flowing eighteenth-century curls, it looked for all the world like him. I smoothed its marble profile. By gentle stages, stages even of delight, I should lead us both, I to my avowal, and he — to his Etruscan.

Before I left, I paused to look out of my high window. The night sky stood at perfect cloud. Yet I shivered. Perhaps love makes mad only the completely normal.

In the club, he stood up as I approached his table. I saw his look of puzzlement; I had expected it. "You've changed your hair again!" he said. "No, that's not it, you've had it done the way you were wearing it when we first . . . ah, that was sweet of you. I always thought too, that it was redder that day, but I could never be — "

We sat down against all the clashing, to a slow rhythm of our own. He stared at me closely. A nightclub table is built to just such a small radius across which couples may lean stalk to stalk, like negligently stacked flowers, or like two matches fused at the top.

I turned, as if on the swivel of vanity, so that he might see, even in that dusky jazz-light, all I was. A wig is the more risky the less swirls and curls it has to conceal the hairline; every wig has to have some — unless it would be like those poor nothings, the toupees; this wig had almost none. It was cut almost flat, like a young girl's or a boy's, almost gamine. Some wearers, of course, can pull out a little of the real hair beneath, to blend. I turned again, to an inner wish — but he was looking at my eyes.

"You're always changing it," he said; "if I didn't know better, I'd say you spent half your time at it." I looked out on the scene before us, where almost everyone else was pretending to be private right out in public.

"Why," I said, "I'm in the habit of . . . wearing wigs." For how many weeks I had planned that careful phrase, that gay plural! "Didn't you know?" And when he looked blank — "Years ago, they used to call them . . . 'transformations.' "

He said "Ah, is that it?" and after a moment, "Yes . . . I know that my mother-in-law — but I thought it was only older women — " He was still doting on my eyes, one of his hands, in nightclub manners, with mine a-playing.

And I said, to the same swing-a-ding of it, "Oh not any more, everyone's doing it now."

I grind my teeth now, to think of it, how I put my birthright down there with those others.

Then he said, "Well, I may be sentimental, but I like this one best. And tell me . . . I've an idea . . . I've a suspicion — "

A skin that can't tan can blush the deeper; the hot, expectant dye rose from shoulders, to cheek — to scalp. I awaited him, steadily.

"Now, tell me," he said, "isn't this the *real* one? The original?"

I lowered my face, until that flush should ebb. "It was, once," I managed to say hoarsely.

"And now?" His cheek was almost on mine.

"And now?" I said. "And now — almost. Not quite."

Then the singer, Makeba, came in to sing. "Isn't her head beautiful?" I said. "I wanted you to see it." My wig, pat to my head as it was, felt clumsy. She stretched back her ebony head, that long, almost shaven head which needed no goldleaf behind it, on which there was merely the faintest blur, only a hairsbreadth of difference between it and skull, a head drawn all in one swelling line which completed itself again, into which setting the face receded like a jewel. He agreed to all these points, adding only that length of neck also was a point of beauty — that singular head, like a music box with a bird in it, on that neck poised. And once more, he doubted that ever a Western — And I stretched so that he could see that my neck also was long. And then we rose, to a rhythm of our own, and went home.

"Very good," he said when we were inside. Travel-case in hand, he scrutinized the room as if it were a collection submitted to him for the museum, but I had pruned as close to the personality I wanted here as the most careful grower of dull plants, even among the prints permitting myself only that commonplace Cranach nude, the high oval of whose forehead flows endlessly from her other nudity, back, back into the dark. " — very good, but where's the rest of you?"

I thrilled to the roots of my danger, like a cat in her suit of fur. "What do you mean?"

He put the case down, teetering on his heels, as if he were here for forever. "Come, come," he said, "anybody talks to you for ten minutes knows you draw your imagery from some other world than the one you look like — I got it the first ten minutes I saw you. And it's certainly not this one."

Never before had I been wild enough to dream him into those alleyways I had assumed I must give up for him, seeing him there at best like some large balloon in the shape of a philanthropist, which I might perhaps tug after me, on tour. But now, I stretched my neck for him, delirious with his cleverness.

"Yes, like *that*," he said " — and then you'll say something with a joke at the back of it, or a pun even, that I can't catch. But there's no joking to this place." He surveyed the room again, scanned the books with a nail. "Ah, I begin to see," he murmured. "For the other 'workers,' eh, as you call them. Your fellow workers. That avocation of yours, that I can never quite believe in."

Yet he was marrying me. My legs trembled toward our pleasure, like some girl of the *trottoir* married by a young roué for her purity — which she has. His hand strayed toward the sugar-cheap marble bust of the English jurist, the ripple of his mouth turning down.

"He looks like you," I said. My voice tremored. "That's why I bought it."

He shrugged, smiled, and said, "Sculpture with curls? Or *beneath* them? D'ya suppose they were his own, powdered? Must say he doesn't look too honest."

Oh, he was keen. Somewhere, a little lady, sitting quiet back there in her altogether, had observed this, adding gaily to herself, "all as it should be, invisibles on both sides." I smiled back at him. "I haven't been to *your* place," I said.

"Ah, nothing there," he answered. He was holding the bust to the mirror, its profile parallel with his own. "Guess I carry my crimes with me," he murmured, mugging at himself like a man sure of only a few hearty blemishes. Then he put the bust down, smoothed his own crown where it was tan-bare, and sighed, in the bluff way men can, when they refer to that — fact. "Uh-oh. Soon."

"Soon!" I echoed greedily — what lechers hope makes! I pushed him toward the bathroom, left towels in his hands, turned on lights for him. "In ten minutes." And I went into the bedroom and closed the door.

My vanity there was pillows. There must have been dozens piled in rows against the headboard, all of the tenderest fabrics for hot-weather nudity, in all of the softest aurora tints — dozens of small pillows all cut to the same replica oval, so that if a head had a fancy to lie there in its own altogether it would seem in any mirror opposite to be lying half in a camouflage of repetitions, or if it sat up, to be rising in the midst of innumerable crescent convexities of itself. Egotism — or beauty — always tends itself most saddeningly in the boudoir. And that was the way I meant to appear, to rise for him, no rubicund Titian rosy-packed in her own curves to the forehead only, but calm crescent of the earliest hour, a Western Aurora.

I embowered myself, taking up a mirror. On my lips I left only the faint vermeil one finds on the lips of bisque dolls, for whom, as they sat bare in the shop, I sometimes felt a sororal — ah now, leave that! But I added more eye shadow, knowing from experience that our so perfect orbs, when left unshaded below that other high oval one, tend to occupy more of its beauty than their fair share. Then I stripped.

He was a gentleman, and gentlemen do not knock. More than that, he was a courtier to the end — or almost. What had he expected of me, other than those innocent capers for which the maribou and the veils might be bought in any bridal salon? We were to marry, and with the respectable zest of the song-of-the-week, he wanted "all of me" — but perhaps not quite so much as he saw. He uttered my name. Again and again he uttered it. Then, in a whisper . . . "You didn't . . . you — " Then he came forward. "But . . . my darling!" he said then, ". . . you shouldn't have done it. Not even for *me*."

Already I knew my mistake, made from the moment I heard him at Knoller's, from my first wig, from age thirteen and before, flowing endlessly back. Any mystery or hope I had made of him — it had all been in my own head from the beginning. But women are slow to unfreeze from their own legends. So I sat there, the draft cold on me in the hour of my only avowal.

"Don't you see how artificial it is?" he said. "Unless it comes from the culture? Otherwise — it's . . .

[35]

depravity." He forced himself to look at me, even tenderly. "My dear," he said, "there's a difference between art and life, you know." He sighed. "But women never see it. They always overdo."

And though I held myself upright in silhouette, meanwhile repeating inner aves to Cimabue, Ghirlandaio, Piero della Francesca, he never said a word about the Western world.

Then he carefully turned down the light, and came to bed with me. He was a gentleman, even if one interested only in statutory nudity. And I think now that he may have had his own wistful legend of me that I violated: either that I was not all I should be — meadows! — or most romantical of all, to the rich — that I was poor. Perhaps, and this is hardest to say, I was *his* vagrant.

For in the end — I'll come to that. But then and there, hell had its furies, and I my vengeance. Men know earlier and better than we what the razor can do and what it can't. I waited until we were fully entwined, then I rested the crown of my head — which his hands had avoided — on his lips.

After a moment, he shuddered, but I held on firmly, moving it only to caress. And after another moment — though strong nostrils indicate what they will to the contrary — we were parted. Willy-nilly, a small sob escaped me.

"Oh my God," he said, not in ecstasy, and even through the dark I could see how he was aghast.

[36]

Then I rose, locked myself in the wig closet, and stayed there throughout all his protestations — a weak opinion of which we both shared — until, at dawn, he at last left me. Art and life, was it? I had taught him the difference.

Three days later, attired in a new Beehive-with-Double-Guiche, and carrying a spare, I left for Bangkok, telling myself that I had good powers of recuperation, perhaps a hairsbreadth too much humor ever to find my solution in *ars amoris* — and two more weeks of vacation. And who should know better than we of the Agency that when people lack love affairs, or pressing money ones, they turn to a study of the ethical world?

Just before I was leaving, the switchboard rang to ask me to take delivery on a package. "Keep it for me!" I snapped, but the doorman said "No, we can't, Miss. It's come in an armored car."

It was the picture that we had both wanted, from Knoller's. I saw the tremendous justice of this, that I should have what so suited me — and what I hadn't paid for, so dearly. But there wasn't time to open it, so I locked it up with the wigs to keep them company, and didn't read his card until I was well out, on the plane.

"Forgive me," he wrote gracefully, "and forget me. I am a dilettante."

Ah he was clever, clever enough even to speak the truth about himself — though I should have phrased

it differently. The half-bald often are. Later on, in
the hotel, I meant to send him a cable of acknowledgment, then thought better of it and settled for a
postcard on which I wrote obscurely, and may never
have sent at all. "I have seen them," it said. "The
monks of Bangkok."

They walked the streets in the early morning in
their orange tunics, going from house to house with
their begging bowls, young boys to old men; a man
could shave his head to be a monk at any time, could
leave his marriage, his children, his aged, and people
would understand his reasons; indeed it was expected of every man that for at least once in his
lifetime he would live hairless. And agreed, they
were beautiful as they walked the dawn-hours with
their concept. And their heads (though merely
shaven), when met at any angle — the high twin-
domes of the forehead brooding toward the welkin,
or that sweet rear haunch above the neck muscles,
nakedly working — when met at any hour, these
were golden unaided, of themselves. But monks
though they were, they were men also, and though
some women can study up ethically to be anything, I
am not one of them. Now and then, I glimpsed the
lean-headed, black-garbed widows, but after all, as
yet I hadn't had their successes either. And finally,
there were the common people, denuded merely to
be sanitary, which I already was.

There remained — if I were to insist on a group
solution to both philosophical problems and practi-

cal ones — one simple course I had never considered myself temperamentally suited for, which however, via an awkward incident in the hotel swimming pool, was brought again to my attention.

At certain hours the pool, a handsome one surprisingly free-form for the East, was deserted, when it was my pleasure to float on my back there in equally free meditation, reviewing the temple-shaped lamps which bordered it, and other more distant pagodas. Actually, the Thai civilization was in many ways also a heavily hatted one — rooftops, headdressed goddesses, dancers — and I found this mentally very supportive. What at home seemed the inexcusable doubleness of the world here seemed merely inexhaustible, and — oh blessings of travel — not my burden.

At these times, due to my having only a spare wig with me, I wore bathing cap merely, one of those shaggy rubber flowers, silly thing, but with a chin strap that buttoned securely under each ear. It is also germane that on this day, the bathing suit I wore was black. For, as I floated, quite suddenly I was jounced, splashed, dived under, sent upright and grabbed round the waist by a man who said, "Tell by that cap you're from the U.S. — *hi!*"

It was my fleeting impression that he was one of those pink-eyed jockey-types who might be either in the opium trade or a representative of American business; it was my firmer one that he was drunk as blazes on gimlets, not frangipani. I batted him away, but he hung on, saying, "Come on baby, don' wan' drown you, jus' wan' see more of you," and binding both my wrists with one of his hands, he tore off my cap with the other. And there we were, treading water vis-à-vis.

Right then and there in the water, he crossed himself. "Omigod, sorry Sister!" he managed to say before he clutched his own head and turned tail. "Sorry omigod, Sister. It never entered my mind nuns went to bathe."

Dressed and downstairs again, I saw no trace of my attacker, but there was now a party of French nuns on the terrace, their enormous, paper-boat-shaped white coifs in full sail. They were several tables away, but in a sense we took tea together. Is it indeed a beautiful arraignment, I asked myself and them, that one in which the skull is first adorned with itself and then forever hidden? I thought of how it must be done, that holy barbering, in community, in gaiety even — a bride. But almost at once I answered myself, hearkening nearer today than I knew. No, even in community, even in communion, I said to myself, it would be an ugly baldness, not a holy one, that tried to hide its birthright under the coif.

One more incident of my tour might be reported. Under the hotel's porte-cochere, a wide advance of steps led up to the doorway. To the left of these, against the façade of the building itself, a line of pariah dogs always rested. Thousands of them, it was said, roamed the city, since it was forbidden by Buddhist law to destroy them — though the police reduced their numbers on the sly. These particular dogs were smart or discreet; they had sought the better part of that public safety whose gradations — from park bench to lamppost, from the outer doors of churches to the underside of bridges — are known to strays the world over. And just as I went up those steps for the last time, one of the dogs — not the mangiest but with a few bare patches — keeping his head on his paws, the way dogs do, rolled his eyes up at me, unmistakably me, and slowly thumped his tail. Dozens of other travelers were going up and down, and to my certain knowledge he and I had never met before, yet he lifted his coattails to me, as it were, in signal.

That day, of course, I ignored it, and continued up the steps of the Hotel Erewan in Bangkok, with exit visa, passport and other credits necessary to the upper parallel, intent only on packing my bags and my conclusions. Half an hour later I had done both, after the fashion of most vacationers. These people here, I told myself, were foreigners, working out their destinies according to foreign reasons; despite our common plight, neither their religion, their bereavements nor their lice as yet were mine.

So I skipped back home, not unfrolicsomely on the way, unlocked the wigs and recurled them, un-

[41]

packed a picture and hung it in the wig closet, put away my pillows and one wig forever, gave a brunch for some colleagues, after which I spent the night on the wharves, sharing my Aquascutum with I-don't-know-who, who was harmless — in short I went back to being myselves. And there I had been ever since — until yesterday. And to con it all over in memory had taken only as long as it takes to fly from Logan to LaGuardia. Brahma itself comes more slowly.

When I disembarked, I tried after all to leave the kit behind, stowed in the overhead rack under a blanket, but the second stewardess came from the rear and handed it to me, shaking her head like a coy goddess — "Tchk, tchk!" I agreed with her estimate of me — "Tchk!" — ran down the ramp, passing two women carrying familiar boxes, and caught a cab which deposited me at Rockefeller Center at 2:48.

Standing in the entry to the Morgan Guaranty, there was a woman not carrying one, but wearing one. It was the best of its kind, every hair human, delicately Aryan and singly sewn, but she had been ill-advised on the streaking, which was contradicted by several small tufts of reality she had coaxed out at the sides. I even knew her procurer, who turns such cases over to an assistant. Under my stare, she reddened, then bridled — there's never much finesse to these liars-without-cause. I waited coolly, until I was sure her eye had certified my carefree, blown strands as being dumpily my own, then I murmured, "Next

time, get Duvoisin himself," and swept on. Let them
cover the earth, these towhead triflers, layercake
beauties, fake Marie Antoinettes who will never
know the guillotine; they would never catch up with
me, who had, as it were, one more head up my
sleeve.

For meditation, there is no place so pure as one of
the patrons' cells in the safe-deposit vaults of a bank
like the Guaranty; the silence whines on diatonically,
set to a combination whose tumblers never fall. After
transacting my upstairs business in a gay welter of
powers of attorney to attorneys, and notary seals
each as firm in design as one large drop of blood
from a cardinal, I went downstairs to the vaults. The
men there greeted me profoundly, like butlers
trained to be grandfathers, or vice versa, and I them,
in the proper responses — over the years we had
trained each other well — and then I took my long
box, of the usual raggle-taggle of certificates and
costumery (which I meant not even to open), went
into my cell, and sat down.

Though the vaults also have a powder room which
might be recommended to wandering duchesses —
chairs Louis Quinze, soap Roger & Gallet, and as far
as I had ever known, never another customer — I
had no intention of staging anywhere within these
precincts my recognition scene with myself. But in
this air, thick with the dead-storage promises of
thousands of keys, I ought to be able at least to settle

on the punctilio of my new life — was it allowable to carry money with me from the old, and what kind of portfolio? Tramps carried kerchiefs on sticks, or used to, sailors their duffel, and so forth — what would be classed as strictly O.K. and necessary for such a vagabond as I? Some of the strays I knew toted gear which was surprisingly personal, like the beggar who carried a bus conductor's coin-gadget — that was it, let the personal be my law! But for the time being I must give myself a little leeway; it would be a shame if, through the overscrupulous zeal of novice or convert, for want of a fiver or a kerchief, I should end up in looney-bin or pokey, instead of where I should be, afloat upon the marts and purlieus, quietly on view.

I sat there for some time, daintily ticking over my little etiquettes — and goodbyes. Say goodbye to R. and Gallet! — where I was going, and in what guise, I'd be lucky to get past the matron in a Howard Johnson's. Say hello to the life of honest dirt, where hot baths are for kings or Salvationers, and every amenity except air has to be fought for. And say farewell to the romanticism of those who work among the poor with their hats on. Admit that the hardy maintenance of my birthright would entangle me in a thousand ruses and stratagems to which my present one was child's play. Accept the fact that honesty requires the most artful dodging of all.

In the *tara-tara* of that thought, bugled through these halls where everybody else was hiding something, I stood up and almost saluted, hand on curls — but managed to bring my hand down again, empty. Not yet. One more place to go — and one more little white lie wouldn't hurt me. So, though my curls burnt my fingers, with that in mind I was able to leave the cell, go through the little ceremony of the key, and walk past my grandfathers the way I had walked in — having kept trust with the Guaranty Trust.

As a reward, I suppose, I was allowed to catch the next cab immediately. But the minute I heard myself give my destination — the office of the attorney to whom I had already given so many powers of — I knew my own weakness. How often I had seen it in the profession! — how those who are merciless in self-criticism often feel enough absolved by it to stay right where they are. True, I had business with George, but after that there must be no more offside destinations. Cringing there in the cab, I came to grips with the one power I hadn't delegated away and couldn't, the one little estate of dull memories, cranky habit-grooves and old private nosepickings, that was locked in my brain forever and is the one which keeps most people from revolution — the power of home.

Matter of fact, it was George who helped me on and away, merely by being who and how he was; in the years to come I shall remember him as we do the last person we saw on shore.

In appearance, George is attractively speckled (with gray, of course) — a silver fox in pepper-and-salt suiting. One doesn't shock George, at least verbally. As with most conservative lawyers, the bulk of his files records a steady round of those good little Czerny exercises which practice money. But George's absorbent manner — that of a man who has gone through everything from divorce with mayhem (if only by proxy), to the problems of setting up trusts for the most secret illegitimates or monsters — is guaranteed to set the putatively criminal layman at his ease.

Behind this limber crime-side manner, he conceals a personal family life of the most Euclidean convention. If I could have depended on this alone, I'd long since have told him my secret, thereby acquiring the comfort of a sounding board, and yes, perhaps a little legal flirtation across the already admirable image he has of me. But his vanity — which certainly would have been to reply that such as I weren't at all new to his experience — until yesterday would have offended mine. The need to be unique dies hard with those who already are — and how to get out of *that* corner with sincerity will be my worry from now on.

"Cruise, eh?" said George. "Archeological — you pay to dig? Or once round the Greek isles before the engine explodes? Or a schooner for suckers? I know you."

And how I counted upon it! "Tramp," I said. That's all — I left the rest to him.

"My dear girl." In George's eyes, I can always see how I look to him — a pleasant sensation, even yesterday. "Tramp steamers went out some years ago. They all have tile baths now. Any that would take on passengers." He squinted at me, and I could see myself sitting on the axial line of his binoculars, a small client of charms just right for the afternoon tea-break, but not as tidy as usual. "You're not thinking of doing a Birdsall?"

"What's that, George?"

"She crewed it. Round the Horn, and the crew never knew she wasn't a — until . . . Let's see now, what year was that . . . ?" He leaned back, intent on bringing in Birdsall in the happy, duckshoot way he always brought in all such citations.

"Oh, no, no." I lowered my lashes. "Not in this partic — not in my situation. I just want to — get away from it all for a while. And though there's no reason for us . . . I mean, for people like me to be anonymous, I mean, incognito . . . I mean of course we already *are*. But it'd be kind of fun."

"Ah." He twiddled with satisfaction. "Us."

I said nothing. George does not leer, and I did not blush. But from then on, our business went with dispatch.

"I agree with you," he said, in process of changing my will. "Ernest doesn't need it. Not he." His disapproval of my brother is based on what he believes to be E's exhibitionism. In time, I shall wonder — and perhaps hear, from a distance — what he will think of mine. "But it does seem a shame that a girl like you can't find a better beneficiary than the Seamen's Institute."

"Oh, I could — " I said. "There's a friend — but so rich already."

"Oho," said George. "I mean — oh no. Not in that case." He beamed at me. "Rich enough already, eh. Sure you don't want to change your mind and let me book you on the United States Line. Get you a seat at the Captain's table. And for, er — any companion, of course."

Just then, the secretary brought in the tea-things. George's windows are high, located in a cozy circle of other enormous buildings nestling round their view. There was a freckle of sun still on the harbor, and from within, the sense of lucid well-being that comes to one, toward end of day, in business offices dedicated to some furnishment which has been running quietly and profitably for a long time.

I envisioned myself at the Captain's table, on my head — which I would hold a la marquise, with the creamy arrogance of those models who know themselves to be the impresario of some extraordinary fashion — perhaps the narrowest chaplet of gems, custom-fitted to be worn banded Indian-wise, across the forehead. For, wouldn't I do better to strike a blow for my rights from the topmost purlieus of the upper parallel, instead of grinding away at my own moral behavior like some sidewalk artist, or from even farther below?

On the Shore Line, for instance, on the west side of the tracks somewhere past the outskirts of Harlem on the way to Port Chester, a large sign always caught the eye, as it had mine only that morning: Madame Baldwina's Bridal Salon, so help me God. Though it was probably merely the ornate fancy of a lady named Baldwin, its possibilities had always amused me, a railside salon of the imagination, never to be patronized except in the mystic flash of empathy as I passed it, but its clients all in my category, all, like me, crouched in the ultimate creature-skin. And now I saw myself, a sudden bride from that salon, rocketed out in the name of my patronne upon the clean, savory, hot-bath-and-massage world of fashion promotion: Madame Baldwina model photo'ed at the Fontana di Trevi, at the Colony and on a bicycle in San Luis Obispo, Miss Baldwina at the Opera, at a first-night, at a Fair. At the Captain's table. Or taking tea with her lawyer.

"What's so funny?" said George.

"They run color ads of the fashionables, don't they?" I said. "On the U.S. Line."

Just then, the secretary made one of the squashed noises given forth by the free and equal of the democracy, to remind us that they are. Celebrities —

she'd often seen them lined up at the rail on sailing-days, or coming into port. She'd even seen my brother. And at her picture of him, the small, clean whirlwind of the morning bore me up again, high enough up — or low — to see that if I joined him, in the world of fact-exploitation where he waltzed with his image, I should merely be upholding the single standard of Myself.

"No?" George said. "O.K., have it your way. At least you've cut that dreary job of yours. Why a girl like you . . . I never. Let those women I've seen you with — let them do it — spinsters who wear *Femme*. Why should a girl like you wear a hairshirt for the rest of the world?"

Such references always give me pause. I raised my lashes, short ones tinted but not added to, as I must so often have done everywhere — in hope. "A girl like me, George?"

He smiled at me. "A golden one. I always thought so." George had a very Edwardian father — who often thinks for him. I smiled back at them both.

At the door, he even patted my shoulder. "Give you any trouble," he murmured, "just you run to papa." I stood still as a totem, and let him do the waltzing and weaving. To deceive, as I knew so well, one often need merely stand still and let other people's conventions do the lying. Otherwise, I couldn't have got him to make all these arrange-ments so blithely — but it was for the last time.

Perhaps he caught an ave atque vale echo; so many of the Edwardians were poets, or Latinists. "Listen," he said, "it's spring, so even a lawyer can say it. Gather your rosebuds, honey. You're one of the few women I'd say it to. Go on and do it; live a little. Just don't lose your head."

Do nuns, on their last novice afternoon, make puns? What could I do but kiss him and hope that this would help him to remember, when he came to judge my state of mind at the time, his own last words to me? And then I said goodbye to him and all the offices of well-being. And then I caught the last cab.

Why is it that when we return home unexpectedly soon, doubling back on the lone prowler of last evening, the stumbler into clothes of the early morning, that we seem to smell the prowler just left, on whom we even seem to be prying? I stood on my own threshold, one of a life already repudiated, and already so nostalgically dear to me for its angel-pains of good or bad, that even to shut the door behind me was an act of dissolve. Then I went round the windows, letting in the last tender shoots of sun and air. The place was to live out its lease in dust covers, and if I hadn't returned by then, my man of so many powers was to use one of them to pack it all off to the warehouse, where, as long as paid for, it might rust for my return under the best possible preservative conditions for sentiment, a little town of life in one room, among so many others of the same. (I had once paid a chance visit to the Manhattan Storage; like a tour of Pompeii, everything sooner or later is grist.) And on the new roads to come, if ever I needed a conundrum to put me to sleep, I could meditate on the odds of my returning to rescue it.

So now, after my morning's hard work at discarding goods, money and other irrelevancies, there was very little else to dispose of, except — the crux. I had kept cut flowers about, but had never had plants, or close friends I must board them with. The air here was only mildly impregnated with the damp, lily-pad affections of some of my co-workers, mostly those whom George had taped so shrewdly, plus a few livelier echoes-in-stereo of the married ones, women of such bursting mental health that they exhausted their families in the expression of it, and had to get away now and then with the girls.

Going down the hall to the bathroom, I had my sharpest moment of — what? The hall is four feet wide, perhaps three times that in length. Nothing hangs there but a few dim lithos. To the right, almost brushing one's arm and looming toward the eyeball as one passes, there is a high lacquer chest, dark and ungainly, put there because it will fit nowhere else. The light is poor. In short, it is a hallway, with no emotion of its own. One goes down it mindlessly, thinking of other things, or of the room at the end of it. Yet when I started down it yesterday I had to stop, whelmed, mourning exactly those unmarked moments. I could have wished for a bundle of them, an old cluster, to take with me. The power of home is in the unmarked moments. My shoulder, my soul, fitted this groove. Is this commonplace? Since I needs must follow the ordinary at a wallflower distance, I have no way of knowing.

Then I went to the wig closet. I knew all about my feelings here, a half-lifetime of them having brought me where I was, so had my answers ready, and experienced no pang. I had come to make my adieux.

The quality of the wig closet is intentness, less ordered than in a laboratory, not as cluttered as a beauty parlor is, but more desperate than in church. Its aims are smaller. Sometimes, when I entered and stood before that long line, I understood, for an ancient, frightened pause, the Old Testament's fleshly fear of idols. There exist wigblocks whose smooth, oval headshapes have been vulgarized with bright cloth covers on which faces are even sewn, simpering masques with patchwork lips and sequined eyelids. Mine are all of the simple, natal wood, their only face that same planed abstraction of one, like the frontal of a casque, which serves them all equally for countenance. All have therefore the same blind, downward look which seems to know the service it performs. They are without obligation to be female. Nevertheless, they are demure, enough so that if one could attach to each block a body molded in its own spirit, I have often thought one might find oneself with a fair replica of the little lady who sits within the skin.

As I faced them, eighteen in all, I remembered the two who had refused to be discarded, and taking them out of their box, set them beside the others. They were none of them in the state I liked them best. Suddenly, I whipped off all their wigs and cast these aside, in a pile. (My sentiment toward the wigs themselves is clear enough; close though we are, I have for them the same feelings I harbor toward women with hair.)

Then they faced me, lyric abstracts of the human head, even almost the poem of it, but too much the appendage of human use ever to be sculpture, and being all alike, one sad step away from art. I suppose that is what most idols are. I stood there for quite a while saying what I thought was goodbye, long enough until I understood what I was really saying. Hello.

Oh larks and gaiety! — for that's what it can be, sometimes, when we finally desert everything we have, in order to greet everything there is. Did you never wonder how it feels to be one of those — the men who walk out of the door one morning natural as life but are never to be seen again, at least not in the proper places? Or perhaps one of those whose unlaid ghosts are still reported — the owners of puddles of clothes left on beaches, of the ownerless

car, left for all to see, on a bridge? I often used to
wonder how it felt to be one of those — the de-
campers. And now I have a notion of how it must be,
even for the wife-deserters, the fathers of five who
tiptoe out and over a back fence of broken bottles —
how it feels for all those who light out and start
walking the underside of the pavement, upside
down, like a child's drawing of Chinamen on the
lower rim of the world.

Glee — that's what it feels like. Half of it, of
course, is for the stone rolled away from the neck-
bone, but the other half is the glee of running. Queer
then though, how they'll still give each other little
helping flips of the hand, or sit, though silent, in each
other's company — for the fire perhaps, but even on a
warm day, as if each saw the same, funny, handmade
grail in front of him. Or not really. For I never met a
manjack among them who didn't believe he was
running toward the facts.

Rough champagne, that, and the price is high —
but it's the drink we're made for. On the fizz of it, I
went round gathering up my portfolio, while the
door to the wig closet, a silent choir loft looking
down, remained open. I chose toilet articles, at first
trying to stick strictly to a philosophy of need, but
that's not to be had for the asking; in the modern
world, what is need? I would be taught it.

I took a plaid car-blanket of consoling Scotch
warmth and color, and a change of inner and outer

clothing — unfortunate that the lightest and warmest should be cashmere and other silky telltales — to supplement the sturdy undergarments, slacks and stout shoes I had already donned. (If the vagrant is often dressed too warmly for year-round weather, it's because Aesop is a liar; it's not the ant who knows most about winter.)

To these I added a head-scarf (for colds) and then, thoughtfully, one of my old turbans from Cooksley. Even nudists must be practical, and I would in time have to get my living. Did I mean to beg, steal, or wash dishes? — here again it came to me that circumstances must be my moral instruction. (It's so hard to remember that just because one is running toward the facts doesn't necessarily mean that one has got them — or ever will.) And at the last minute I added a short veil of gauze.

The veil was connected with a slight ambition of mine already burgeoning. For it's entirely possible to be both honest and frivolous, a role that men deny exists, of course, since only women are perfect for it. It seems to me in no way odd that Paris, the goal of so many professions from eaters to lovers, should also be mine. Not that the underside of New York is to be despised; a vagrant who has got even as far as one of its boroughs has come very far. But from books I've read, Bohèmes I've listened to, there appeared to be no place for one of our sort quite like the banks of the Seine, or perhaps the barges. (After that, with

[56]

the onset of age and maybe wisdom, perhaps
Athens.) And though from now on I mightn't look it,
I knew myself to be very conventional really, if not
at heart, as they say, then perhaps from the bottom,
where the conventions are more normally located.
So, for Paris in the spring, I carried gauze.

Then I shouldered my strap-bag. An Abercrombie
pouch of fine leather and canvas, veteran of picnic
weekends of yore, it made me look all too much like
the *poule de luxe* of vagabonds, but time would soon
darken us both, tanning us not with holiday but with
the truths of exposure, like bright pennies in water.
Then I turned to go.

And then, it was my heart — which I have, oh I
have — that rose in me, bubbled like a drain in
which too much had been cast, but stood by for
service as hearts do, imperfectly beating. The door to
the wig closet was open — what use now, locks? —
but I had intended to go straight past it. Had I? Had
I forgotten what was hanging there? Have you?

It hung in its own niche, well above the wigs, or
did until yesterday — Knoller's picture, Knoller's Picasso. I have sometimes suspected it to be of rather
too small a size for the general run of those of his
works classified as of that period of his known as the
"bone period," but even if it shouldn't really be a
Picasso, neither the donor nor I had been bilked.
Surely the blue behind the figures is his blue, the
shore they sit on his pebble-crazed, wind-eaten

shore, the canvas itself only a pause between two claps of wind. They are his figures, the two terrible bones with knobs for heads and an eye between them. Sad clasped, they sit against the blue, and how human is bone! Who, in their bleak sight, would call for hair, or even flesh, to cover it? But in their lower parts they are joined, as if to remember where flesh was quickest and bone may still be, in the parts where love is made. Sad clasped they sit, against the blue. I took off my last wig, and laid it before them.

Though I might stand there until Christendom come again and all the bones did rise, I should never be as free, white and equal as they were. They were art and I was life, with a hey nonny nonny — I won't say for which of us. Meanwhile, though I had already disposed of them by bequest — to Ernest — I found that I didn't want him to have them after all, or not without me. Someday, they and I might present ourselves before him, for such a family reunion as is given to few stars of the cinema. In *Californie*, on my way to Paris, perhaps, on the odd beeline which is the zigzag one must expect of roads that were to be as open as mine. Meanwhile, I would take them along with me for my personal, the very psalm of my life, as sung by somebody else.

I found they wouldn't fit in the pouch as yet, someday perhaps, as needs wore out or were discarded. I wrapped them in a chamois — useful for windows, should I go out washing them — and put the picture in a Harvard book-bag, which it fitted exactly. Then I had a glass of water. Then I ate a chocolate. Then I went to the bathroom, came out again, shouldered both bags, and stood in front of the door. Scarved for the journey, but otherwise rather cold about the ears, my head hung down, a donkey awaiting its Giddy-ap and Gee. I stamped my foot at myself, but the door did not open. And finally, I was able to open it and then shut it behind me, first tossing the keys inside. So I abandoned the roost for the road, the long, sweet domestic life of "What-I-feel" for the sterner shake-a-leg of "What-I-am." It was nothing like my young dreams of going for a cabinboy — though it might turn out to be the most masculine thing I've done yet.

In the elevator, luckily self-service, I was nervy. All of me felt weak and exposed, like an invalid up on his pins again but not without a suspicion that there'd been more to the operation than supposed. I got past the doorman without difficulty.

"Taxi, Miss?" he said, but of course I declined. Ever since a certain event in both our lives he had been particularly respectful; unless my scarf slipped, he would remain so.

"Cheerio, Duggins," I said. "And watch out for more armored cars."

It wasn't until I boarded the subway that I realized those words had been my last address to the first-class-with-loungeseats world I was leaving. I decided they would do.

It was just dusk when I got off in the neighborhood of my case-load, the locale I'd chosen to start out in. Honeymoons might be nothing more than unveiling, but all unveilings were not exactly — well, yes it was cowardly of me. But I couldn't afford to start out on 42nd, a street under constant patrol for all the exhibitionists that were there already; yet in the subway, where the bashed-in people will tolerate anything, I would never be noticed at all. Later on, when I was really in practice, in that happy future when all would be ordinary again — at least for me — I planned to work my way uptown, even to hare off to the better country resorts, at weekends. Right now, I found myself not really conservative, but choosy. Which means timid. I suppose there's no exactly right place to be reborn in, but I've not done so badly. This neighborhood is ruined, but lively. If the same is said of me, I shan't be sorry.

One way to start the ruination was to get rid of all the extra money I had by me, all in packets thin enough to be slipped under a door, but when totaled, rather a sum. The teller had been horrified; banks so disapprove of cash one would think they hadn't got any. It's credit, of course, that makes the planet whirl smartly; cash is for scum. I was scummed to the ears with it. It wasn't that I still kept any special brief for the poor-in-houses as people; I had long since been aware that their mechanisms of kindness or the reverse were at best about the same as anybody else's; nor was I even any longer romantical enough to expect any change in that area in those of the viaduct, though I preferred them. But the difference between rich and poor isn't only cash or credit; it's scope. To my professional knowledge, windfalls were scarce down here. These were my reasons; the facts were, that even in the most decently uncovered heads, the poor can still be a damn headache.

I had a modest forty-five cases in my load — and they were all special, of course; that is, they were the ones I knew. As the evening darkened, and I toiled up one after the other of the tenement stairs as I had done so often before — one couldn't trust the mailboxes, from which even government checks were regularly burgled — I carefully kept myself from any sly satisfactions of charity that I might have dragged with me from Tudor City, but couldn't help being merry. I delivered to dark fanlights only, but had all their habits so closely by me that few return visits were needed. Now and then I stopped at a stall to have a slice of pizza or a knish or an ice, and almost every other one of the old hallways still had toilets — the whole evening was like an old household whose marvelously simple conveniences I was learning.

In my envelopes were bills of small denomination, in sums ranging no higher than $250, the limit I had set in order not to have the matter noised about, or to alarm the receivers, to many of whom good fortune was never anonymous or gratuitous. On most, I had written something not instructional, just enough to show good intention, and that it was for them. And on each, I tried to hit a note median between their fantasies and their needs — "For Rosie's piano" — she would never play it; "For Mannie's funeral" — he had already had it; "For luck" to the gambler; "For the patent leathers"; "For the pimp" — since after all, wasn't this what I was doing for myself?

As I went up the stairs to leave the last envelope — for my old client whose politeness was always to warn me away from her own bedbugs, I felt relaxed and yet a-tingle, greased for the long birth-canal and ready to slide into the light. The fact was that my scarf, a Liberty tie-silk, ill-chosen to stay on a bare skull, must have slipped its knot sometime back — later I found it caught inside the lining of my Aquascutum. But I was by now too tired to notice anything but that the old woman's door was dark, or to recall that her insomnia went without electricity except when visited. Her hearing too, was as sharp as the rats she kept at bay with her broom handle. I had no sooner stepped to the door, hand not yet in pouch, when the door opened. She knew me, almost at once, I think. But she was a resourceful woman. She didn't want to.

"A dybbuk, a dybbuk!" she shouted — which

wasn't likely to wake anybody in this house of Italians. Then she shut the door. But she was lonely. A minute later, it opened a crack. "If you are a dybbuk," her voice said, "touch the mezuzah on the door above, it will rest you, then leave yet, hah? If you are the worker from the agency, come in."

Her kindness to dybbuks melted me. I entered. She was ready for me, already moaning and ritually gnashing. "Oy, what an accident. What to happen, Oy."

"Not . . . an accident." Confiding was new to me. "I — we — " I don't know where I meant to begin.

She opened her eyes. "Those Italienisches. A *fight* maybe?"

I opened mine. Could she think they had scalped me? "No — no — "

"So, ah-hah, I thought so. Those crooks," she said. "You go to the priest," she said. She hissed it. "Go to their priest; he'll get it back for you before they sell it, such a beautiful wig."

I wept then, from shock.

"Oy, dolling," she said, rocking me. "All of them you have, so byudifful. Musta cost a fortune. Those crooks."

We were on the couch. I noticed she no longer bothered to warn me about the boggles. It's no trick at all to come down in the world.

That cheered me. I dried my tears. "Does everybody know? That I wear them?"

"I don't know wedder from everybody?" she said sulkily. "Me. My friend Mrs. Levin the beautician, she said it. And maybe we told Mrs. Yutzik in Hester Street, she's an invalid."

"And the Italians," I said. I thought it best to leave it at that.

When I was ready to go, having found the scarf, she scuttled off, telling me to wait, and returned with something wrapped in newspaper. "Put on to go home," she said. "And good riddance to it." She struck her own brow. "Such connections it has, in the mind. Wait till donstairs, hah. To put."

It was a sheitel, the ugly wig worn after marriage and meant to be known as such, shiny red-brown and bumpy as their Friday bread. That reminded me. Down the block, yes, there the baker was already at his ovens, it must be half-past three. I missed having a watch, but the disciplines must begin; later I would be rewarded for its loss by a spryer time-sense, the total loss of one that comes to those without watches. For every so-called loss, I could look forward to other gains.

I went in to buy rolls, and while the baker's back was turned, dropped the sheitel lightly on a tray of the breads which would always tell me, newspaper-less though I might be, that it was indeed Friday. I did this in imitation of my friends under the viaduct, who saved as queerly as anybody who was not on the move, but when they threw something away, did so with an indefinable elegance. Then I retraced my steps to the old lady's house — she would have to chance it on the mailbox — and dropped in my last delivery, whose inscription read: "For a couch."

On the way to the viaduct, I looked back at what was already yesterday. Yesterday is a village now, already a place so little on the move that I shall always be able to look back to see how all the life-stories have worked out, including mine. I moved on.

The viaduct is a particularly coveted one, having at its opposite arch a public convenience, far enough away so that there is no smell, even downwind. Fires are not allowed by the city, of course, nor sleeping, but several niches in its fin-de-siècle architecture are excellent for either. The neighborhood, too, still a family one though on the fringe of the peculiarly livid hells of the Bowery, attracts a remarkably high class of loiterer, few winos, no hopheads, no feelies. Old men with Joaquin Miller beards still abound in the world; young ones "on the beat bit," as they like to say, are setting up their new generation of the same (though I sometimes think it a shame to waste all that sincerity on such little experience); then there's usually a scattering of Puerto Ricans who haven't made it to Harlem yet or are making away from there, also now and then a crone or two (princesses-royal of the paper bag and always the least chummy), and here and there a tart. The Seamen's

Institute is nearby; though we see none of them here, it lends a churchly presence. Down the alley is the all-night Chinese restaurant. Altogether, in the gradation, not a bad setup for a novice.

As far as I could see, no one was installed there yet, certainly no fire, though that might be due to time of year. Down here, the obscurities of night become doubly soft as one approaches the river, doubly tender, as if hiding only babes in cabbages. The cop's last round was at four, but some of the nicer ones rarely made it — what they don't see don't hurtem. Doesn't. (Hmm — why not? — don't.) Out in front of the arch, some yards distant, there is a public bench, under a lamppost.

I sat down on it, weary, not gay any more, but not sad either, perhaps in just that state of mind when the noumenon stops nagging and not-so-blind young phenomenon gets its chance. Or perhaps it was just that in the bad sections of New York the old lampposts are so beautiful. This one hung its long, graceful urn against a sky dark as the inside of a much larger urn that enclosed both of us. It swung itself a creaking inch or two; get born, sister; get born. The wind that blows my shore is a small one. I wished for the society of my kind — those under many hats in many places, or at home in their most private wigs a-sleeping. I wished for my brother. But my crusade is the smallest also, running to a company of one. So it was just here, that it began.

Without scarf, I could feel how the light shone gladly on the forehead that keeps us from the apes they say — with the help of that even whiter, high naked oval above it — below which my eyes, without their false shadow, must be gleaming beyond their fair green share. I didn't need a mirror to unveil in, or swear a resolve to, but arched my neck like a swan's, shifted my scalp, reserved ear-wiggling for a less sacred moment, but let the breeze play like a sixth sense around them. When the time comes, it's like grace or death, perhaps. When the time comes, it's nothing much. Except that you don't always hear the cop behind you.

It was my first formal confrontation. I spoke first, as one always should to the establishment, and very distinctly. "Good evening, officer."

He gasped; he must have thought me a boy. It was rather a comfort that he didn't gasp more than he did. The New York police have of course seen everything and twice around, including the man who regularly walks lower Fifth Avenue in tam, perfect Glenurquhart kilt — and lace panties — or the beggar who stands in full beard, a costume out of Parsifal and a smile like a sneer from a pulpit, in the West Fifties, on wild-weather Sundays. At the thought that I might be classed with these, I held my heritage the higher, if wanly. What could I say to him, except as it has been said by plumpers-for-the-fact eternally: Officer, it's mine.

[67]

He drew nearer; my uptown accent had stayed him, but he came on nevertheless. "Wotyer doing here . . . Miss?" Nearer, he looked puzzled; perhaps he had caught a resemblance. I decided to declare myself, thinking that this might settle it. One learns.

"Don't you know me, Officer?" Delicately I framed my hands over my brow, just enough to bring out the face.

"Why, *Miss* — " he said. "Why, Miss — " Pity crept over his cheeks with its mild, coronary pink, and I knew I was lost. "Why, it's the lady from the agency. Whatever are you doing here?"

"Oh . . . just . . . taking the air. Lovely, isn't it?" It was no use; he was already backing away from me.

"Work done now, eh? You'll be getting along home, eh. Not a place to hang around this late, even though we — " he gulped — "know you."

"Oh, after a while. It's the first night of spring, you know." That *was* a mistake.

"Mmm," he said. "Live far?"

"Not very far," I said. I was learning, but one last try. "Officer, would you oblige me in something?"

"Why yes, of course, Miss." Eager. "Get you a cab?"

"No. Just take off your hat."

Without the hat, I could see that his hairline was well receded, almost gone. He was a middle-aged man, not bad-featured but heavy-headed, with small ears and a flaccid, white jowl; when that faded red line had finally left him, he was going to look, from the front at least, like a polar bear whose grandmother had come from County Kildare. Yet, if he took off his hat, no one would run him in for it.

"Thank you," I said. "That's all."

"And you're welcome, dear," he said. "Fine evening, indeed now. You enjoy it, love." He crooned it. "Stay right where you are."

When he came back from the call-box, of course I wasn't there. Ruses and stratagems were all coming on as well as could be expected. But I was still an apprentice, on a warm evening. I had left behind my precious Aquascutum.

From the side-window of the Chinese restaurant, where I ordered a pot of tea, I watched the officer come back and go away again. Under the lamppost, in the pool of light where I had first asserted my birthright, the bench was bare. Except for the loss of my raincoat, it seemed almost as if it had never happened. I was as used to this "except-for" brand of kismet as anybody else on the planet. But I found I had no desire to live by my losses only, no matter what graceful interpretations I might make of them. Oh, I had so much to learn, and at this hour, all of it stared at me at once. Is there a preferred style to be honest in? Was it quite the rough-and-ready to do a bunk on a cop by having tea?

The restaurant, empty now, was just that sort of land's-end in which people so often sit at the end of their own wits, or at the beginning of them. The tiled floor, of the pattern of beer parlors in the days of Nellie, the Beautiful Cloak Model, had had scratched on it all the intervening sorrows of grime; the walls had once been painted in landscape, in those peculiar Corot-forests of varnish and gravy-fleck down which one could never wander far. Yet, over even the dingiest of such Sing Wu's, there hangs always a certain paper fantasy, something of fans and kites, and out there in the kitchen, moth-plaints of a language not cognate — not the worst kind to hear in the background when one is taking stock. I wasn't out to be a heroine — I wasn't serious enough for it, I just wanted to be ordinary. But I didn't seem to be Freudian enough for that either, at least not to the police. From his croon I was sure he was a man who knew all about how to be. The ones who do, they're always the enemy. Watch out for good will, sociological and psychological — all those of kind intention who would kill me for my own good, either by keeping me in my place or sending me back to it. Oh, up with the coattails and all that, of course, but it was a long way between signals, and already the second day of spring. And right now, at the hour before dawn, when the blood-sugar level is lowest, I needed to be told that taking something off could be as positive and worthy an act as putting something on — a policy our children aren't bred to. I could make use of a fortune cookie that said it.

When I shouldered my bag again, and put down the money for the tea, the two Chinese who had been chittering in the back came forward. Though the old Chinatown *tongs* that brought them here were said to be dying, recruits like these still arrived regularly in the poorer eating-houses. Two pale boys with coarsely shining hair, lips swollen with youthful serenity, and inquiring nostrils, they had waited upon me together, teaching each other how to learn by serving a single pot of tea in unison. Three weeks ago, perhaps, they had been in Taiwan, and their landscape still walked with them; I could see their bent backs sculptured in the field. There is a kind of innocence that hangs for a long time about people who leave their homeland early. They don't know precisely what events, which people in the new land, must be called strange.

And now once more, as these two ovaled up to me, bowing and curving, I was reminded of how, in Bangkok, Oriental gesture had always seemed to me to be fluently addressed to a point beyond me, its immediate object — as if all but me were chorus to a play whose main roles were being played elsewhere.

Surely my tip, modestly suited to my new status, couldn't have caused all this twittering. "English?" I said into it. "Do you happen to speak any — "

In their seashell language, they deprecated themselves, humbly powerful. Grow grass they could, or set a table of teakwood thoughts in this wilderness, or mend the sky — with a gesture — when it was in danger of falling — but no, they spoke no English.

When I finally understood them, I couldn't speak either. For, finally, one brought me a small wooden salad bowl, cupped my hands round it gently, as if valet to a personage, and even more humbly set my money — the quarter for the tea also — inside it. So, once again, I saw myself in somebody's mirror, and this time I smiled.

As I left, tucking the bowl under an armpit, I pressed my palms together and bowed over them, glad that my travels had educated me enough to say thank you in monk language. In their final flurry of bows, they seemed even to be pointing me on my way — to the viaduct.

When I looked back, they had stopped bowing. One leaned in the doorway, staring out into the neon-thumbed night. The other, head bent, studied the carnation reek of our gutters. And I? — I'm a silly woman — I tripped along mystically, thinking of all the new roles my new head might have in store for me. I thought I saw the pattern of the life it held out to me and all wanderers, a life that was all episodes, through which I was the connecting string. Though these were to fall tangential as snow, it was my fate to unite them. Is *this* ordinary?

And is it customary to stand still on the pathway and give thanks to the general scene that you are in it, uncomfortable as you are? I did that! When the wild jackass coughs by night in the desert, bringing up all the poetry he has chewed by day, that's what it must sound like. For, think of it, I had never before felt the absolute hilarity which comes of knowing that one's equipment is equal to one's intentions! Face to face with the diorama of where I could go — (and would) up to and including captain death's table — my head fairly dizzied itself. I turned it yet once again — this large, superbly bare fact on my shoulders. I wanted to thank the boys back there for being my signal. Then it came to me — that I had been theirs. And that this was the inexhaustible doubleness of the world.

When I got to the viaduct, I found out why they had urged me here. One of the niches was occupied, by I-don't-know-who, rolled up in my raincoat. I sat down next to him, pushed my pouch against the wall for a pillow, and considered him, snug in my coat there, if it rained.

Would he lend his half, in that case?

Does the future of the world depend upon it?

And would I steal it back for my own, when I woke?

Does the future of the world depend upon it?

Along toward dawn, he roused himself, stumbled toward the public convenience, didn't get that far, but in a gentlemanly, sleepwalking way, managed to put a fair distance between us. Behind him, the night went up one lucent step. Head bent, he looked from

[73]

the rear as if he were praying. I appreciated his courtesy.

So, when he came back, I said in a cheery voice, "I'll lend you back the half you stole, eh?" Bleary-eyed, he nodded, without another look at me, and so we lay down to sleep, back to back, in mutual trust, or a draw. He and I were harmless.

I lay for a while on my elbow. Before me, the ordinary phoenix-fire of day was rising. We are born, we live and we die; crouch and adore. I watched the waterbugs streak like lizards from the Chinese restaurant, the men stride like catamounts, from plain doors. In the inexhaustible doubleness of the world, are there signals everywhere, wild as grass, that unite us? Or must we unite them?

What is imagination? I used to think it was to struggle against the facts like a fly trying to get out of the cosmos.

Come, you narks, cops, feds, dicks, railway police, members of the force everywhere! Run with us! If the world is round, who's running after who?

In the cold of morning, I wrapped a scarf about my ears, but loosely, no deception, and lay down to rest with plenty of leeway until well after sunup, when the first rounds are once again made. Children can learn to be bald. And so to bed. What is imagination? And so to dream the answer, which I knew of course, but could never say. And so — I was born.

The Last Trolley Ride

I

THERE were once, *said my grandfathers Jim* — this
was years ago — two sisters named Emily and
Lottie Pardee, nice girls with pleasant enough small
faces and ankles too, but they lived at the end of the
town, and nobody could keep them in mind. Ever
so often, people would suddenly remember this fact,
that nobody could keep the Pardee girls in mind, and
this would last for a while, but then that would pass
out of mind too. Their parents had been the same
way; they would be at church and at church suppers
like anybody else, and they were invited to weddings
too, like everybody else — and afterwards, when people were going over the affair in their minds, they
could recall very well that the Pardees had been
there. But scarcely anybody ever recalled afterward
that they ever got to any of the really important
places where things were transacted, like last minute
phone calls to come to supper, or small meetings in
the vestry or grange, which hadn't been arranged for,
or even picnics and pajama-parties, when they were

young. And when the parents died, leaving the girls
with the neat little house out of town to keep, and, it
was said, a tidy little sum to do it with, alas, it was
soon clear that they had been left this other inheritance too. For one might have thought that lots
of young sparks would be drawn to that cozy fireside
— even two at a time, since there were two Pardees —
and that with the automobile coming in as strong as
it was, there would be a double wedding out there in
jigtime. But it just didn't seem as if this would ever
happen. There are some people born to live at the
end of a town.

So what the sisters did, for they had a sort of quiet
spunkiness between them, was to have a bay window
cut into the front of the house, and they set up to
boiling fritters in it and selling them to eat. The
fritters were wonderful; sometimes they came out of
the hot fat like a butterfly and sometimes like a
blossom, but always they were miles lighter than a
doughnut, and gone quicker. It was a queer kind of
eating experience and a delightful one, but the kind
more or less remembered afterward as a one-time
affair, without needing to hunt for it again. People
tried to be faithful, sometimes sent their children for
a treat or came by themselves for takeouts, but a
taste for fritters never seemed to settle itself to a time
of day, enough for regularity, and there's no doubt
that the best business is regulation business. There
was one young man named Jim, he used to come, it

began to be said, some said always when Emily had her turn in the window; some said no, it was Lottie — but the truth was he couldn't stand sitting in that lighted window, at the one little zinc table and wire chair. If they'd had two chairs and tables put in, it would have helped, but they hadn't. He never thought to bring a mate with him at first, which would have helped matters too. For although he was a man, and even in those days, even without many automobiles, men could get about easier in love than women, Jim had a trouble not unlike the sisters. He had been born at the other end of the town.

I don't know that this needs much explaining, even now. Though in his case, it wasn't a question of railroad tracks but of barges. On the Erie Canal, there was always a part of barge life that was family and respectable; the wives and men too could go to Sunday church and did, though it couldn't always be the same one, except now and then through the year. That was the difference. For the people of the up-state region — whether they live forty miles from a great lakeside or ten from one of the fingerling small ones — are a landlocked people. And they want it that way, though in those days, without so many cars and planes, you could see this clearer. It troubled them too, maybe, that their state was so various. The people in the towns and farms of that nor'nor'west part of New York State had given their hearts to the chasms and ravines mostly, and there wasn't much left over for water. Winters, on the short, overcast afternoon when the dairy farm ponds were frozen, of course they skated them, and summers, many a canoe was flipped onto the smaller waters, of Honeoye maybe or Canadice or Hemlock. Otherwise, they sat in their tight dark winters, which the women hotted up with calico, and stared out at the numb farmland through air the color of an oyster; nine months of the year there is never much sun in those towns. Or they drove out to look at that hill near Palmyra where Joseph Smith the Mormon had his vision, or past Oneida, where a community had once hammered silver into free love. And when the barge people came to town — even though a family of these might get to their church several times a year, and come around steady as a season year after year, married as close as anybody and maybe as schooled too — the others looked at them with eyes that were the color of oysters, even though maybe they themselves had never seen one.

At least that was the way it must always have seemed to Jim, as a barge child. At times, he even went to school on land with the others, but although he had a last name like some of theirs, and once in a while even kin here and there, it was the once-in-a-while and the general scatter that did it; he might as well have been a gypsy, or one of the Italians from the wineries which had made a little Italy out of the

hills around Naples and Hammondsport, who went
to the Pope's church. Or else it was the water itself
that was an invasion to the others, the farm and
townspeople, even though it was the found money
that worked their truckland and wetted their apple
orchards and humbled itself to carry down from the
flour mills at Rochester and the knitting mills at
Cohoes, and everywhere else. Summers of course,
there was more roister on the canals, and the farm-
boys meanwhile had their noses hard to the grind; if
a runaway farmboy was lost to the barges, he might
as well have been lost to the Indians in the days
before these were all on reservations — for the
amount of hullaballoo that was made. And even
when Jim's parents retired to the little wayside house
by a bit of water, which was all that was left for him
to return to after the war — and where else should he
come? — still, for all the changes that had been
made in towns and roads and people, there was still a
lingering difference between him and them. A town
that size always has people who remember its gyp-
sies. And even if not, as Jim would often tell the mate
he'd brought back to share the house — war-
buddies, the town called them, quite fondly — even
polite as the town was to him now, and even if he
could see for himself that what with the house-and-
lot developments going on everywhere (this was
nineteen-twenty) that if he stuck around long

[81]

enough he'd be an old-timer himself, still *he'd* be the one to remember, even then. Barge people had their own way of remembering, half land, half water.

It was all in the names of places, the difference between them and the town, he'd now and then say to the mate, across the deal table in the kitchen of the little house, after the dinner they'd cooked quite neatly, and just before they got down to talking, night after night, of what kind of business they'd go into after they'd saved enough from the fat, steady but no-account jobs they'd got into but wouldn't stay at — no, not they. Jim's mate had come from the coal mines of Pennsylvania out of Lancashire, England, when he was thirteen, and farmland was to him what the canals were to Jim — though to him, by an even more cut-off memory, it was of what he'd never yet had. He didn't talk much, either of what he had had or he hadn't, but he could sing of it now and then — and he could listen.

"It's all in the names of the places," Jim would say. "There isn't a square foot of New York State that isn't within spitting range of some kind of water — falls, rapids, lake or creek — and within day or two range of the great waters. You wouldn't think that this inland fever would hit some people this way." But it did. It was his contention that, let a New York town stand back only ten miles from a river and it called itself something like Middlesex or Woodsville, or Horseheads or Roseboom, or Painted Post. Nice enough names, but landhungry, in a town way. The canal names were another breed, wider and lazier, lots of them Indian or classical, or marined from elsewhere, or simply practical, like Lockport. "Three canals of the inland waterway, there were at the beginning," Jim would say, in the special, swinging voice he kept for this use, though the voice itself knew that this was nearly nineteen-twenty-one, and the canals were done for. "The Erie, the Champlain and the Oswego. Then, only as far back as nineteen-oh-three — I was already eleven — they even voted to make way for the new big ones, to hold barges up to one-thousand-ton burden. Troy to Waterford, along the Hudson. Kept the old part of the canal, up the Mohawk, to Rome. Rome to Clyde, the canal takes in the Oneida and the Seneca. Rivers, mate. Westward from Clyde, it goes up to the Niagara, at Tonawanda. I was born Mohawk to Rome, just outside of Oriskany."

"Aye," would say his mate, who had never seen big water, not even from the troopship. By the map though, pulled out on the table for his education, he could see well enough that Jim had barely escaped being born outside of a town called Whitesboro one way and a Middleville the other, but he never pointed this out, nor the plain fact that many of the waterway towns had a landlubberly enough sound, and many of the mountain ones a wail of water. To him, the hills around here looked enough like Scotland to be Yorkshire, and he knew well enough what it was those hills — and what they had or hadn't in among them — could do to people. If people here aimed to keep their feet out of water, no matter how much they had of it, it could be these powerful hills alongside, and so wild in the beginning, which had been to blame. Bears and bobcats, even now. But this he never said, either.

And all this was only after-dinner talk, transportation talk really, of the kind men always get involved in, even if it's only how long by bicycle to Maple Avenue. Though, in their case, it was preparatory to whether the joint business would or would not be what had begun to be called a "garage." Nor did the town's semi-distant way with newcomers, or even with its own, much bother them; if the two of them spoke between themselves of such things, it was only a joshing way of admitting to each other that in certain ways they were shy. The town was a nice, pert one, with most of its clapboard in good condition, plus half a dozen mansions made of the small cobblestone that used to roll up on the shores of Ontario, and a lot of silent money in the sock — also not too many grannies with hair on their chins, or other characters left over from before the world got smart. Indeed, Jim and his mate often spoke of it, how it was in the air here that the young people were in control — or soon would be. It was just the town to make your way in, once you knew your way.

And its name, if not the most dashing, still had bits of nature in it — Sand Spring.

Shy they both were, though they went everywhere with the returned soldier's bold air of still seeing the world, and Jim's mate blamed his own hanging back on his not being American enough yet. He was away on one of his surveying jobs, the two three times, three it was, Jim walked over to Pardees — which meant two miles to town, one and a half through it and four on the other side round by the lake shore. Oh yes, there was a lake in Sand Spring, but back of it there was a rack of hills, making the town a sort of valley — though like all the valleys in this double country it was only a temporary valley, between the hills holding their breath and the waters holding back. Anyway, it was a lot of walking just to appear casual, but to bicycle all the way just for fritters went against the grain, though it was the ideas of the fritters that got him — set up in a bay window for all to see, four miles out of town! — plus a little bit the idea of the Pardees.

For if those girls had been left none of that family business to go on with, it was no fault of their being women; women had run that sort of business before, just as women had now and then done the same on the canals. Whose fault was it, certainly not those two girls', that there were getting to be no livery stables any more? It was something along this idea he had in mind, as he walked. He'd had women before; he wasn't *that* sort, and except for just now he wasn't even particularly backward with those you could marry. But at the moment, as he told his mate later, he was thinking of how the barges were going down, dropping down, derry-down, into a lock they'd never get out of — and how the livery stables were already almost gone. Those who lived by the wheel, or the clop-clop of a horse, or even water, were always being flung offside, and in the moment that whelmed them there was maybe a kinship between them, or maybe a warning, like those failed families that sometimes get together on a back street. Even for a bargeman, who always has some allowable thinking time, Jim had been a dreamy one — not that the mate was far behind. But these thoughts were not unlikely ones for any man who was thinking of setting up the first auto agency in a town, and nearly the first garage. In any case, this was how it came about that his idea of the Pardees wasn't pushing at the fact that they were young women.

It was three times he went there, no, four. The first and third times he went, there was a crowd of others, or some. On the first time, as he told his mate later, they were just the selection of people you might see lined up outside a mechanical Dairy Cream bar on any roadside today, not important, you understand, but interesting just the same, and always about the same. Only this time, being of the neighborhood, some of them were in the house. But all the rest of it

[86]

was queerish, or maybe just for those times, or maybe — just for him. She had set herself up in the bay window, you see, stove and all — and although there was nobody sitting just now at the ice-cream-parlor table and chair, she was going at it, wire basket dipping up, and a great bowl for the finished ones and a sweep of the powdered-sugar canister, and then back to the wire basket again — never done. And it was at her doings people were standing to stare. It was Emily. Lottie was back there in the front room, which had been cleared of its rugs and put down with lino, and she was flitting about as much as a roly-poly like her could, serving, serving from a tray and probably eating too, and — it was hoped — taking people's money, though as he came up to the sight of it all, it was more like a lakeside party — that moment of a party when if stopped to be looked at, it is queer.

As he came up to the house, the sun was going down on the lake in front of it in a stew of orange, and behind it there was that grim, green light which always comes from lakeside woods at this hour — on a fuller body of water, one of the great ones, the light would have been blue. Or brown-black, he thought, though he hadn't the idea quite yet how much the actions in the bay window reminded him of the way barge life was always moving, while the land and people stood still.

But what he did fancy to himself in passing was

[87]

that what she was really doing, up there, was making the minutes into fritters, and when he went inside to taste them, he didn't change his mind. "Quicker'n a minute," one man inside even said, as he poked his child in the stomach. And it was true, just like it is true of some ice-creams even today; these fritters, really a kind of puffball with barely enough outer crust to hold them in life, were gone almost before you could taste them, no matter how many you had — and the child, after a number of them had been popped into him, opened his bewildered red face and began to cry.

Jim went outside again, to look. She was still making them, cooking up the minutes in that same hard and perfect way women will do handwork of the silliest pattern, as if it were important and admirable. Since that sort of handwork bored him stiff, he went away that time, but not without casting a look about for the stables — until he remembered that these would have been in town of course; this house, wintertight as it might be for the climate, would have been their "other house," as people who had gone into town business here sometimes said of the home farm. Or else the Pardees, having lived long enough over the stable while the money was being made, might have bought this house later. Still, it was odd he saw nothing in the small barn, not even a wagon, or even on the back porch, a bike. But as he cast a look back over his shoulder he saw that they had the electric, even way out here, though they had waited until the very last of the real light to turn it on; people were sparer with the cost of it in those days, when it was still new. But now they had snapped it on, and with that, the party look was gone, and the place was only one of those halfway businesses with a porch still to it, and people going away from it to homes that were still all home. Enough fritters had passed by. It was time.

The second occasion he went there, he told his mate, he sat in the window at the table, there being no other customers except a neighbor child and baby brother she was taking care of, this being a choice house to hang around, of a Saturday afternoon. It struck him as a bad sign for business that nobody else was thinking of it as lively enough for their Saturdays, but he said nothing of this, though this time he and the sisters did get to talk. Lottie was the older by four and a half years, and just as clearly the baby; not that she was whiny, just that she hung back waiting to be told whatever, meanwhile nipping from the trays. It might have been thought that she was waiting for a man; some women eat like that when they are. But from what came out later, it would seem that, round and soft as she was, and always waiting to be told, and pretty in the face as a kewpie doll, she was one of those women who aren't made for sex but for sugar, whole igloos of it, plus all the tender emotions — crabmeat patties to curd-cream — of a richly wooing diet; it wasn't her fault if some man mistook the pink deepness at her neckline for something more than a roastbeef flame. Emily was quiet, but in a livelier way, and skinnier, from taking the lead. She had a small face, with two furry black eyebrows she was lucky didn't meet in the middle, and large eyes that were either farsighted or near, but so vague they kept you from seeing how neatly her hands were going. From what the town said when it bothered, he knew she was lucky all round — she was the sort of girl who no sooner does she declare her intentions to go for a nurse, then her parents come down with bargain-rate last illnesses she can learn from, right at home.

So there he was, sitting up in the window, all asses' ears and beer etiquette, not knowing whether he could look into the back kitchen, where the sun was still shining in from that side of the house, it being not yet one o'clock, or whether he ought to stare out at the lake. The two Pardees were enclosed in high aprons that tied at the back and dropped from neck almost to ankle, a kind that must have been bought at bazaars before their time and used to be worn by ladies when they served at such bazaars or went into the kitchen to oversee the maid. Here in the shop, these signaled that the Pardees were at your service, but ladies still. The kitchen, despite its moment of sunshine, was full of that kind of doubletalk; was this an outright shop or just an amateur operation; was this all just a pretty moment of fancywork for two healthy girls who didn't have the nerve or the need to get work in town — or were the Pardees poor? And was this Sand Spring 1920, or Sand Spring 1898?

The sun dazzled a dishcloth, then moved ahead dead center over the roof, casting the pupils of all below into temporary shadow, and the whole sweep of the house, from bay to kitchen, into the nice gloom which came of knowing that in a short while the glare would strike the lake. Everything was live and fresh enough here, nothing dead or eerie or shut-in; not a yard from his nose, on a rack near the special stove which had been set in the window, other dishcloths and towels smelled of the outdoor ozone they'd been dried in — it wasn't that. And if he wanted surety that he and the Pardees were alive and ticking, there, in a big iron pot as big as a cannonball, there were the minutes bubbling — it wasn't that. Lottie was making the dough and Emily for the moment was feeding the sweet scraps to the two children as if they were puppies, though her job was to tend the pot, lifting and lowering the wire strainer, putting in the raw and taking out the finished, then a whisk of sugar and onto a plate, and all in a rhythm that knew beforehand how fast he would swallow; four minutes from now she would be once again at his side. If he ate five dozen of those things, he would still have eaten nothing but an hour.

He watched everything, nevertheless. For the life

of him, he couldn't have told later which sister had informed him that the proper word for what he was swallowing was baynays (from the French of a recipe come down from a Canuck in the family) but more commonly called bennies — or which had told him that the stove, a tall affair of many intricate drafts, warming ledges and ovenwells, grandly crowned by helmet-and-spike, and painted aluminum, was called "Bismarck." Like many a couple who lived together, speak up as the sisters might separately, the effect was of unison. And why not, if their experience of living was to be as unison as the Pardees'? Why else was it that if he asked some of the foolish questions in his head — which he wouldn't, being already stretched enough by asking himself — or even if they answered willingly enough, which they couldn't, they would still tell him nothing he and they didn't both already know? For the doubletalk that was in the house wasn't theirs or his; it was the town's — and the fact that they all knew this already was what, past or present, made it a town. Otherwise, as he asked his mate later, why would it be that a man could come back from such a Flanders of a war, plus two years of schooling the war had gifted him with after, and still wouldn't know his way in life any better than the town's way, *once he had plumped for the town?* Out in the world back there, as back as far as Europe, for instance, he had known his way about with women,

at least to the point of sleeping with some of them —
and even before. Right now, as the mate well knew,
back East, not four hundred miles away on the
coastline of this same state, the world was full of
flappers whose dresses wouldn't reach Sand Spring
until Sears, Roebuck chose to send them maybe two
years from now — and whose manners would take a
lot longer. Or was it that, back there, he and Jim had
only passed through? But once Jim himself had got
here, no matter what he might do — and he wasn't
fool enough to think that a lot *didn't* get done here
— the town would still make his conversation for
him. By his taste for a freedom outside it and his
stubborn wish to be of it, it had neatly returned him
almost to the state in which he had left it, a watery
young'un, Sunday scholar in its visitors' pews, or at
its back-row desks. Coming back to it was like coming to court must have been, in the old days; the
gossip here was like a sieve. Yet the current was
bouncy enough, returning him up down like a fountain, or a woman, for his help and his chastisement
too.

He closed vainly on another bennie fritter. And
found that Emily and another dozen were at his side.

This time, though she moved off almost at once,
like a good waitress or a thoughtful lady-of-the-
house, they held a silently monitored conversation.
The town said (in him and for him) that her father,
in his eagerness to make ladies of the daughters of a

father in the horse trade, had kept her from all the things that even ladies were now doing. And in her and for her (no matter what Jim himself might say to her) the town would pretty well have taken care that she address him in one or other of the characters it held proper to him; whether it would be as a war-buddy, or as a fellow with his gypsy life not yet lived down, he'd soon see. Though surely, some pioneers in conversation broke out of the preordained.

He was to do it, too, though not then and there. By the time he'd swallowed up eight of those things, he'd remembered the vague kinship which had walked him over here. However, the decline and rise of transportation, and people with it, was too wide a subject for the soda-pop chair he was sitting on, so instead he put his fork in fritter number nine. He'd been using a fork all that time, finger freedom not having been offered. Then, at number ten, the sun, just as if it hadn't been inching along all that time, reared over the house in a leap like a horse and struck the lake to white, and splashed all five of them inside there glare-blind. It was over in a second. Outside the bay window, a line of red cannas he hadn't noticed before started up like an audience, all tongues. On number twelve, he spoke. "How you folks get to town from here?" he said.

He got several answers, this time slow enough so he could assign them to their dealers. To his surprise,

Lottie spoke up first; he was to learn that she could speak up smartly enough when it was a case of what she couldn't do, though the full extent of that wasn't known even to her, until the end. "Never could get the hang of a bike," she said, looking modestly down at what would someday be piano legs and hams, but right now, though bursting, were still young peony fat; he judged her to be about twenty-four.

Then Emily spoke, in a thoughtful way. "Shanks' mare . . . might be . . . the best." He wasn't sure whether or not this was a statement, but it was the "might be" which got him, moving away his idea of her away from "one of the Pardees" almost to Emily — the idea of her being a woman, squeezing in between. He judged her to be old for her age, about nineteen, one year younger than the century, he being nine years behind her. The century line was still much in people's ways of reckoning when he was a boy; you watch how it'll be as the next one hoves to.

Just then, one of the next-door kids who were still underfoot, the girl one, spoke up, first giving a swipe to her baby brother for dribbling his sweater on the floor. She had one of the fritters between her small thumb and finger, and staring at Jim, she popped it in and ate it, even chewing as she spoke. He watched, fascinated, it being probably the only time human teeth ever got one of those things. So, her words came to him delayed. "Neighbors," she said.

"Ne-*eigh*bors take them." She drew down her long little jaw, making a face she must have seen somewhere. "Us."

When he got out of there, after quickly paying his fifty cents for all you could eat, which was the arrangement, he stopped at a bend in the road to look back. There were obligations neighbors paid by right, or even goodness of heart, and still made faces over, which their children could copy. This still didn't mean that the sisters were poor. The town said they weren't. They might just have to be careful — which meant he needn't grow a sympathy the pair hadn't asked for, though as their only customer of the afternoon he felt a certain right at least to judge their enterprise. Why it should be a place where he heard the doubletalk so keenly, he couldn't imagine; though in any town there were bound to be such places, he had always imagined them as more private. The afternoon was bordering on rain now, with the swift changes that came to these hilled waters. The stall in the bay window, dark as if it had given up hope of further trade now that the sun had all but gone underwater, seemed itself full of passing clouds. Of a sudden, as if the sun down under there had turned over, and the lake given up an aproned woman, her arm dripping, there flashed into his mind the simple reason for the stall's presence. Those girls knew what the town's verdict on them was, just as he and every soul around each knew of his own. "Nicer

girls you'd never want to talk to — when you're talking to them." Some women wore flashy garters to
keep people looking at them, or took lessons in
coloratura. Those two had done it homestyle, dime a
dozen or fifty cents an hour. It was their bid to stay
in the eyes and minds and thoughts of people, not to
be winked out.

When he got home, he tried to tell something of
this to his mate, who listened willingly enough, and
was moreover a man who never really forgot anything he was told, not anything — four and a half
months later he would look up from his plate and say,
"What's about this Lottie, you once said."

And what about people — aren't the tags and
loose ends and final catchings-up enough to break
anyone's heart? But at that moment the mate was
just in from a trip which had taken in Cazenovia and
Skaneateles, bully towns for auto setups or any other,
both of them, and he was already wild on tomorrow's
trip over to Chenango and Wampsville; if it was left
to him there was a real question whether those two
wouldn't have a chain of dream garages before they
had a real one of them — and a homemade New
York State atlas into the bargain. As for the other
topic; once they had got the map, they lost it there.
Maps take in people like that all the time.

And on the occasion of the third visit, Jim's mate
having gone down the Genesee to two towns just
outside of Cattaraugus which he was sure to be in

love with, their names being Almond and Angelica
— see the map for yourself if you don't believe
me — Jim again went to the Pardees alone. But this
time people, and gossip too, had got there before
him. It was a Spanish War Veterans picnic, with the
families of course, some of the granddaddies being
from the Civil. The Spanish ones mostly weren't even
fair into middle age yet, some of them not much
more than ten years older than Jim. It wasn't the
kind of continuity he was interested in, but it was the
kind a man can't avoid, even though his own war is
hardly in the Legion clubhouse yet, except on the
plaque to the dead.

Before he plunged in, his eye, which these days
was seeing business thoughts everywhere, saw the
place as a picnic grove with tables and docks and
beaches, and even a place for boats-to-hire. Second
thought told him it couldn't be done — except by a
stranger maybe — for it was not yet the town's way
to hire these things out, instead of just leaving them
to be called on, or borrowed (though twenty-five
years later, that shoreline was all cottaged and con-
cessioned and pounded down like a beachhead; as
for the woods in back, the jack-in-the-pulpits had
long since taken their sermons elsewhere). He saw
that the veterans had very kindly brought their own
tables and chairs, and even more generously their
own food, including the usual chocolate cake, which
no doubt could be chewed. White pitchers stood on

many of the tables. Though a few children were straggling untended in and out the side of the house, there was no trade going on from house to picnic; nobody except Bismarck was in the bay.

On his way there, two of the veterans who worked in his factory greeted him. At the door, a woman smearing a child's happy mouth with a hard cloth nodded at him, turning out to be the night librarian where he sometimes went to read. Inside the kitchen, he saw only Lottie, peeping out, not cooking, though there were signs she had been — maybe a batch or two she'd been feeding the children for free. His mind made up at once what had happened to Emily; she had gone to be a nurse. He was neither disappointed nor pleased, recording merely the idea that Lottie was a woman too — and that either sister was more interesting when alone. Together, they were merely a situation. What he might intend to do, he addressed to that — it made no difference to him to which of them, as long as it was only one at a time, this being how his previous experience with women ran. He didn't mind having an experience, in between the maps and the building-sites, even if it risked being a serious one, which in this town it sure would be — maybe it was time. But this day and age, a grown woman ought at least be alone for it. So he smiled at Lottie's neckline, strode over to the table in the window and sat down — lucky he'd had no lunch. After four or five dozen of those things, he

[99]

wouldn't want any, though from the novelty of it and the rhythm of the girl at his side he might be left with richer appetites, like a love potion in reverse. Had the sisters thought of this too?

"Oh . . . but we didn't — " said Lottie, and he stared at her, speaking there as if she were answering him, fat pullet-hands clasped at a chest with a depth curve in it like the beginning of a two-hearted valentine.

Then steps sounded, and with her long, light stride Emily came in; she must have only been to the bathroom, or in the house somewhere. Though she might have been his first choice if he'd been offered one, he looked at her now with some enmity.

"We weren't going to — " Lottie said, a hand out toward the stove, her eyes on her sister. "Were we."

Emily said nothing right away; she had that power, not always an easy one for a woman to have. It gave him time to wonder if the picnic people had angered the sisters into retreat by their not buying, or was it the opposite entirely, that the sisters were too delicate with acquaintances to push their trade? But more than anything, he wondered not only why he never thought of the town's doubletalk as much as he did here, but why he never understood it better than he did here — though from all sides. It never occurred to him, the lake air being as calm as Hiawatha here, and the quartered-oak floor of the bay jutting out so strong upon it with its cargo of housewifery — that its owners might not know themselves why they did what.

Just then, the two men outside who knew him rapped on the glass. Weatherstripped though it was, it was no proof against their sharp summer voices.

"Which one is it, Jim? Can't have 'em both. Where's your mate?"

They kept up a chorus of this, knocking their tin mugs against the house, until a couple of the women came and got them, not without peering in themselves, though all that handwork women do makes them manage their eyes better.

"See what you're in for, Jim!" one of the men called out, and the other man, with a grinning wave of the hand said something too, but the lake air sopped it away. The white gloom of the afternoons in these parts came and settled, temporarily taking away the spring; always in these parts the winter comes and stands for a moment, in any season. The two girls watched it, a land-ghost they were used to, but Jim thought of canal weather, different always from the very land it traveled, the mornings blue with their own business and boat-notions, even in a freeze, or a fog. As for other ghosts, no matter what the mixture of names was around Sand Spring, none of the three saw anything but what was immediate. White people didn't see Indian ghosts. Nor do many in the modern age see classical ones — though those three would have a chance at it.

Lottie, at the glass, peered after the two men. "They must have been rushing the growler," she said.

Jim stayed mum; in addition to his inborn barge-quiet, he'd learned in France to get along by watching expressions. But Emily had already seen his, having picked up that talent right at home.

"No," he said, as if she'd pulled a string in him, "I don't know what it means. Rushing the growler — what's that?"

"You can see he's never lived over a stable, or near a saloon," said Emily thoughtfully and over his head — as if she and her sister were standing in their shifts, talking him over at bedtime. Again, like last time, he had a sense of messages given and taken between her and him, if only by being withheld. She hadn't much of a neckline. No criticism — but the differentiation was going to have to start somewhere. He had a sneaking wish that one of the sisters could have had a sign on her somewhere, such as having the name of some former girl of his who had worked out, or a string of amber beads like his mother's. To trust entirely to luck in these matters had always seemed to him a bit dirty; it was more gentlemanly to proceed from choice.

"Of course not," said Lottie, equally over his head. "He grew up on a barge."

They often talk like this, very literal, very simple — the sugar-people, the fat ones. From which other people take it that they're as simple inside, and what's worse, they take it so themselves.

Curiously enough, though he was thinking of them both in their shifts, it wasn't Lottie he could see best, for all her marshmallow meat, but the other one. He could see her standing in hers in front of him, or even naked, thin and intense, more emotion to her than there was line, though she would have her points of it, and a little knock-kneed, like women with good legs often are. What he couldn't quite see was whether she would be embarrassed. There was a chance she wouldn't be. But what he could see — as clear ahead of him as that the men outside were still laughing and the sky behind them was a mackerel one — was that he would succeed with one of the sisters here. The question was — which?

Does it seem to you that the climate intervenes less nowadays in conversations? In the old days there was more climate of course, you can be certain of that; has to be, to make them the olden days. But surely the climate came and stood of itself more in conversation than it does now; it expected to be watched — a matter of all kinds of lore from skies to a wet finger held to the wind — and it gave you time. He wetted a finger and held it up so that either girl stood to one side of it. There to the left was Lottie, waiting to be told, a ripe fruit maybe, but bunched very close to the bough. And there on the other side was Emily, in her upper lip that willful, deep trough down which a kiss might well slide against duty. Which way the wind blew was plain as his forefinger between them. In the bay window, blank now, the afternoon, special property of women such as these two could well come to be, took over. Mornings were child's gold and the evening belonged to the married, the courting or the social. Night, where it was not for sleep, was for hawks and harried travelers, and thieves. But in towns like these, whatever their names, the afternoons were the special property of the spinster. He squinted at the two sisters along the finger. They would never get separated until they married. They would never marry until they got separate.

"But your *war*-buddy," said Lottie, "he was brought up in England."

He nodded, though only a woman would say it that way instead of just plain "buddy"; still, it showed interest, and as he told his mate later, she was the first to mention *him*. Otherwise, he could see they had no intention of telling what "rushing the growler" meant (though he could guess) or rather, they meant him to tease it out of them in more of these stretched conversations — and suddenly he had had enough of it; he had passed over that hairline divide which always hovers between what a man can take of female activity, and what — no matter how lively his motives of love or rape are — he can't.

He'd had all he could take of this fancywork that placed the heaviest burdens of meaning on the lightest nothings, especially since he saw that Emily, making one of her quiet moves that somehow always drew more notice than Lottie's louder ones, was now at the great gray-helmeted stove, which must have a property that most of its kind didn't, of holding heat without showing it. Or, were there any others of its kind?

Now, when a house, an ordinary one by its neighborhood standards, it could be in Sand Spring *or* Flanders, begins to take on a special significance to a man (whether or not he can bear it), so that mere cakes become butterflies and stoves become eccentric or dear in character — and when that house has woman in it — take warning. For, in spite of all this heavy-light business, whimsy doesn't come natural to women; most of the whimsy in the world comes out of the men. Look back on the books you were brought up on; see if I'm not right. Sure enough it was the sisters who had mentioned the stove was christened Bismarck, but who was to say what family historian or politicker had once named it? And who was it was looking at it now, thinking, as he said later, that it was looking right back at him through the grizzle-gray eyepiece of its armor like an old iron eunuch, not missing a thing or a person that came in the kitchen door?

From inside one of its ovens, Lottie drew out

another of those black cannonball pots somebody
had provided this household with, the dark ages
maybe. This time it was a smaller version, of a size to
contain a potion, but on her setting it in front of him
it only disclosed more of those damned yellow fluffs
— he couldn't get one more down him now if he was
blessed for it, or even if he was to be offered one of
the women with it, she as nude as the fritter, both of
them spitted on the devil's toasting-fork. Outside the
window, he saw that the tables were empty, the
women and children scattered, most of the men of
the picnic being gathered along the shoreline, stroll-
ing or in groups of jokers, and he longed for that pair
who knew him to come and rescue him, with whatever guffaws. In the foreground, between him and
them, on the table nearest to the window, one of
their stoneware pitchers reared large, in another and
a realer world. There was no barrier like a window.
Mentally, he jumped through the glass — or the
small Robin Goodfellow soul of him did, and landed
neatly on the cold mouth-edge of the pitcher, just
before it dove into what wasn't lemonade, from
what he could see of those waterside stragglers, but
beer. Well — as he said to his mate later — luckily
he was able to recall that there were still doors to
that house, so he stood up politely enough, though
he may have licked at his dry mouth a bit — and
made ready to bolt.

It was Lottie who leaned across him — to pick up

one of the dainties in the pot. That double valentine she carried in front leaned with her, in fact splitting wide enough to show him, since it wasn't a whore's and her sister was standing right by her, that some kind of mental innocent owned it. It wasn't this that got him.

"Try one," she said, and though he choked a bit, of course he knew that she was addressing the tiny eatable she held pinched between two cushiony fingertips — and wasn't even really offering it either. In fact she was murmuring to it like to a baby.

"Day old, you're different," she said. "Way I like you best." Then her lips parted softly, so that he saw the gleam on their jello-pink insides; then she nipped the poor thing — that's the way he thought of it — between her milk-fine teeth, and it was gone, to what pinker recesses he could only imagine — and certainly did. But just before it went down her, the tip of her tongue came out partway to meet it, nothing gross, delicate as anything, indeed not like a bodily flicker, more intelligent. But it was this that got him.

You are all bound to think of us as a generation that didn't scarcely smell the dark angles of closeness, fleshly closeness, much less speak of them; isn't true of course — how do you think you all got here? Never trust what one century thinks of another, much less one generation. It was only that we didn't speak out so much in a crowd as you do. And you

seem to us like a solid row of tongues hanging out
day and night for excitement, and only getting dry
for it, in all that wind. We see you falsely of course
— as falsely forward as you see us backward. Don't
you think I know that and so calculate my vision of
us both? And when you are able to correct yours that
way, what'll you be? Old?

Anyway, it wasn't too much of a mistake that saw
Lottie's tongue as the liveliest part of her, and
jumped to her quick show of it as to a sexual flicker
more common to other parts, which was where it
took him. Not that he knew yet whether or not he'd
made a choice.

For leave it to Emily, as was learned later, to take
up a moment of surprise, hers or anybody else's, and
kick it further up the ladder. What she did, or he
thought he saw her do, was to leap past him, through
the window. Anyway, she leaned across him, just as
Lottie had done, but without stopping — and without the neckline of course — and continued past
him, her apron skirts in serene sail, with perhaps a
bit of ankle added — a sight of some interest, though
not as piercing. A next moment's revision told him
that she had merely stepped gracefully through the
bay, which opened French-style — but by this time
she was already back over the sill, with the white
pitcher clasped to her, and a smile. And in all of this,
there was no competition with Lottie, though there
was certainly something, just what — he couldn't

say. She set down the pitcher firm center on the table, reached an arm behind her the way queens sit, without looking, and appeared to pick a glass from the air there — unless anyone wished to note that her tidy little rump backed against a shelf. She poured from the pitcher. He was so dry, he would have drunk chicken's blood. It was beer.

She lifted her chin in time to his long swig of it, then bent her head again, tucking in her smile. "I rushed the growler," she said.

Lottie giggled. "It means to go down to the saloon for beer," she said. "And to bring it back in a pitcher. Or a can."

So there the two of them were again, in unison.

Or maybe not. For Emily, pouring him another, spoke singly into it, so that the glass he took held her question as well. "What's your . . . buddy's name?" she said.

Jim looked into the glass before he drank, and it was a long moment before he answered. He was feeling that tickle of terror which comes from a person seeing ahead of him into life-probabilities which nature should have kept him from seeing, and ordinarily does. As his mate and he agreed much, much later, too late to be of any use, it was like looking at a map of the future — not dead cert, but a tour you could surely take — not knowing whether to learn it hard as you could, or to screw up your eyes and run on the double away from it. For there was Lottie, her eyes bright as candy in a curved jar. And sitting at the small table he had just deserted, leaning those heavy eyebrows on her knuckles, that girl who every time he saw her he thought should have been blackhaired, not brown. And here he was, and his mate, bumbling all over the map of New York by day, but — by this other map — not far. Any of them could count up the possibilities; perhaps these two already had. He was struck with the terror of it, and the charm. Two and two — but *which?* — makes four.

"My . . . mate?" he said. The word buddy, for the comic strips, the sob-sisters of the Stars and Stripes even, and for the town of course — never crossed the two men's lips. "My mate's name?" He smiled to himself, a true bachelor's smile, for from the odd-timeness of jobs and even meditation, he and his mate spent more time alone than the dinners they had together, though when these came about, the talk and the silences matched well enough; this was what it meant, having a mate. He let the smile broaden to include anybody in the room. "We're twin-names," he said. "I thought you knew."

On the sill where she had stepped over, a feather rested, blown in from nesting maybe though it was early for that, a clean feather silk-smooth at the top, not separated anywhere, with a fluff toward the pen-tip of it, from some middle-sized bird, nothing fancy, but whose tail nobody had yet put salt on. He smiled at it too. The sisters knew of the names, his and the mate's; there wasn't a chance that they didn't; in a Sand Spring, the structure of the gossip at least let one see what were impossibilities too.

Gently he reached down and picked up the feather. He wasn't a picker-up of pins or a sufferer from any of the nerve twitches that came in about ten years later, but to a boy grown up on a deck, the soil that was so wild and itinerant under the feet of shore boys was always precious, as well as any stray pebble and shot from it. Whereas to a boy from the coal caverns, as his mate always remarked, a clean deck to walk on would have been like silver, and the towns the mate fell in love with, one after the other, were always clean. The two of them were opposites then, not unlike a pair of sisters. And this was enough of parallels, at least for now.

He had no hat on, ever, so just before he bolted, he put the feather behind his ear. "Maybe that's why we came to be buddies," he said from outside, leaning back into the bay again. "My mate's name is Jim."

II

ORAL description cannot touch that spring — and not because it is gone — or that there will be others just like. Washlines left out on its evenings had a mystery, and even to the well-sighted, an arbor in a garden sank back in the twilight like an Italian arch. Projects were touched by it, or people were moved to them. Even the plans for a Ford agency were affected, the way a plain street, with plain maples and horse-chestnuts, is one morning littered with the wildest yellows and greens. And when the householder has swept these away, then down come the whites. It was a time of clearness and short, lovable mysteries, when a man may well be afflicted with a keenness of sight for things he has always known aren't there.

The mate had found his town. At least — after days and days of his circuit-riding under those wind-glassy skies, toward horizons which were one moment riotous and the next second as neat and sharp as a pruned hedge — when he burst in on the dinner-

chops with a statement to that effect, it was clear
that the time had come; he had *had* to find it, just as
much as if a giant traffic-hand had come down in the
road before him, holding up a sign that said STOP
THEN GO. As he said to Jim, if they weren't to let
themselves be chosen, they must choose. In this town
that had found him, there was a house to which was
already attached the means for just such a business,
agency and garage, as they wanted, also a half-acre
of frontage for expansion, also — unimportantly of
course — an owner named Skinner. Skinner didn't
particularly want to sell; in fact, said the mate, the
idea had not yet occurred to the man, but they were
going to get that setup from him — in an honest way
of course — if they had to hire three wolves to blow
him out of there.

"Three pigs, it was," said Jim. "That story is the
other way round. I mean — one wolf. Not even two."
But he had to laugh. The two of them looked at each
other, grinning. They weren't looking in any reflect-
ing mirror. Jim couldn't help knowing he was handsome, a tall, rolling-gaited man with a fresh complexion, whose pink cheeks annoyed him with their
youth. The mate was shorter, though not as short as
he looked, with a chiropractor's neck and arms, or a
pick-axer's, and not bad-featured in a pugnacious
way, but swart enough to keep him always at the
razor, and not above a sneak of talcum on the jowls.
Like many from the mines, he had a fine voice, the

[113]

speaking one too — and he couldn't help knowing
from the women, beginning with his own mother,
that he had a smile. And where Jim's head was close-
shaven enough for a phrenologist, so that in some
lights his blond hair seemed white, the mate's black
crop shot forward in a forelock which made him look
as if he was being pulled along by it — even to
himself. Looking back at them both, they were a nice
pair, part of the grinning being that they knew it.
Slice either of them, and you'd get only honesty,
tempered with need but not yet burnt by it.

"Pigs is pigs," said the mate, adding that Skinner's
house, and certain others in the neighborhood, had
been built by Swedes, a Swede carpenter, and
scrubbed by his faithful fry ever since — or almost.

"What's its name," said Jim. "This great town."

"Names, names," said the mate, but he was smiling. "It's on the main road, of course, but it's just a
section. I don't think it's on the map, really." Then he
leaned back and laughed so hard he had to slap
himself. He jabbed a fork at Jim. "Going northwest,
ask for directions, they say 'It's just after you get to
the Palewater Reservoir, mister.' How's that for you?
But if you ask going southwest to it, they tell you
'It's just about after you leave the Champion Woods
Pulp Company.' How's that?"

"No name," said Jim. "Where in the love of God is
this place? What's it near?"

They got out the map, which spread itself out in

a resigned way. The mate's finger trembled, skipping over the Adirondacks, going due west as if it were a dowser's, then due south. When it found the spot, it could barely hover over, jouncing with excitement. Jim looked at him, inquiring, then down at the map.

There for sure was Palewater, in one direction. And there was Champion Woods, in another. Between them, on the main road, there was a minim of space which when it stretched to human scale must be quite comfortable, though Jim's spirits sank a bit at the idea of its being on the road well enough but without a town to it — of course they had to have the road. But he'd been thinking of some deep green well of a town, up to which the lively motors would come to drink, man-made and hearty, but then somehow fade, fade away again, leaving the place natural.

"Look harder," said the mate. He moved his finger away. There are four directions to a map, after all, and Jim had looked in only two of them. He looked crossways in a third direction, then, following it down, in a fourth.

"By God!" said Jim. "By *God*, Jim!"

A few miles in the fourth direction, there was Oriskany — where he'd been born.

They spent the balance of the night talking equities and amortizations and other money talk which a session with the local banker had taught them quite well, but that night there wasn't anything professional about it except their solemn, joined manner; it was as if they had entered upon an agreed magic dialogue which would keep old man Skinner from selling before morning. Most selling and buying, once it gets past sensible need and projects into the future, is nothing but this kind of personification and magic, with maybe some group madness thrown in. And most bankers even, and businessmen — but that's another story and no time for it, except to point out that Skinner — who promptly became Skinflint in the partners' talk, and must have aged twenty years overnight in the bargain — was actually himself only one grade less innocent than a chickenfarming type, and only about forty-three. Since the next day was Sunday, they drove over to see him. Cars were already well in of course, though still called autos, and had been in for years, and taxis and buses too; don't think the dates are wrong here; we are simply still in the period when they hadn't taken over yet. The mate and Jim had no Stutz Bearcat; they had a Ford. It got them there just before supper, a quarter of five o'clock.

Skinner must have thought they had dropped from heaven, even though they had telephoned ahead. He was the mouse-haired, hysterical type who should have married a big woman to boss him, and maybe with psychology to help him along with his woes he would have, but these were the olden days, and instead he'd married his wife. She was just bright enough to drop children like rabbits, and pink-eyed ones too, just like herself, but she was also the legatee of this house we two were after.

We. But there — it's been understood all along, hasn't it, who that pair was?

Well, to go on, there was the house — and the barn (for it was a farmhouse, and the barn was the greater part of it) — the barn of stone-and-mortar, ledged for posterity and for a sunlight it hadn't quite been able to get that far north, and a seventeen-ninety over the door. The house itself was later, but good too, clapboard, center entrance, double chimneys and a fanlight; that Swedish carpenter had passed through Vermont. There were no Adam mantels but what use would the partners make even of five fireplaces with such a good draw? — and the house was good seasoned wood all through, made to stand, and no plumbing or heating yet, which would keep the price down, and of course, there in front, already let into what had once been the second parlor, was the grocery store and store window — which was how the Skinners skinned along. This would be the partner's office. As for the barn, it already housed a Model T Ford lost in it like an omen, to show how many more of its kind that barn could take on. Outside, there was already one gas pump, and over the acreage behind all, a hill for the sun to rise out of, and across the post road built by the first settlers, a woods for it to go down into. Oh, it was a fine setup that had caught the mate's eye, or would be, once the Skinner litter had been cleaned off of everywhere, the pair said to themselves; there's no litter worse than a bad farmer's, and Skinner, among other things, had been ploughing up the acreage for something. Even the store was half-hearted, with signs the family had been at their own groceries, and tawdry ones too. The barn took Jim's eye at once; it was beautiful.

The trouble was, the place had no need or real reason to be at all, any more; none of it did, not barn nor house nor the land. But how were Jim, who didn't know about land yet, or the mate, who'd never yet had any, to know this — that such a property, in such a place, can pass from hand to hand and still, like an amulet, keep its first stubborn luck attached to it? Even the Skinner litter would be a deception, prompting an industrious buyer to think he was the man to make the change. The trouble with these houses that last is that they were built for nothing but *once* — and for the post road. They last and last, but they won't ever pervert to anything else, not to summer places, because of the road, not to business ones, because of no town. But people are always trying, in their stalls and stores and eateries, and of course anyplace having such a sunup and sundown has a good deal to do with it. So it has come about that these houses on roads without towns are the badlands of America in a small way, just as those great glory holes at the center of the continent — the canyons and deserts — are its badlands in a grand way, land where nothing more than carnival or show, or a surprise of the spirit, can ever be arranged. But these other smaller places — being so random but still everywhere in the lymph and life of the countryside and the cityside too — there's nothing to be done but to spit and to stamp on them, and to start all over again in these new developments, as is being done now. As for the partners, one look at Skinner with that fine hill and all its works behind him, and they were convinced they had come just in time.

A price was quickly agreed upon by all tycoons present, said sum first being tempered the partners' way — by reason of their willingness to take over all mortgage arrears as soon as they had the money to do it, and then tempered Skinner's way — by reason of his willingness to wait. Imagination was therefore left free on both sides, to rejoice in its bargain. The partners, for instance, were welcome to visit their property-to-be at any time, and in the next months tirelessly did so. Skinner, in taking them the rounds of their estate, often pointed out to them improvements they would make, when he was in a large mood, or repairs he hadn't been up to, if he was in a restrained one — to both of which they agreed, like the indulgent landlords they were. Indeed, imagination was rampant on all sides that spring; even the children gathered at the fenceline when the partners left, to stare sullenly at the new owners, and behind them, sometimes the wife too. Skinner enjoyed it most of any, stepping with the lordly pace of a man whose property is wanted, and as came out later, making no more mortgage payments. The property itself needed to do nothing, being everybody's dream.

The new owners themselves worried a little, as they felt the advancing lures of property, heavy and light. As they would leave it, at a sundown, the mate often shook his head over it, looking back. "That woman's no housekeeper," he might say, as he had said that first evening, or something like. Jim, blinking equally in the golden outpour which hid somewhere behind it his watery birthplace, always summed it up his way, never varying. "Well," he always said, as he too had that first evening. "Well, that lets out Sand Spring."

During those months also, the trips to Oriskany — as they had taken to calling these, though they never went near the namesake town itself — seemed to take the place of other close relationships, or rather, to free them for still another kind. The mate, though still traveling regularly on his job, no longer found new land-and-home treasures, or was dulled or sated to them, now that he was owned. He found himself thinking of women again, or at least of kindly waitresses along the way, many of whom were extra kind in this magnolia weather, and it was no trouble at all to persuade Jim to ankle along with

him in that sort of teamwork. The two of them found
that the States were no different from Europe in these
matters, only, in a queer way, more cynical. And
don't be surprised that these matters are mentioned
here. For, just because we seem to be constructing an
idyll here — and maybe we are — doesn't mean that
a man doesn't remember the more humdrum pleas-
ures of such a time, as well. What is an idyll, but that
part of a man's life which he will remember with
clarity for all of it, so that all his years his tongue can
go on touching it, as on a live nerve?

As for the Pardees, these other matters, that is,
other women, even helped Jim remember them,
whereas along the line of the sisters' usual destiny
they might have been forgotten — though how so-
called low women often help out the high ladies
might not be appreciated by either side. But so it
was — and so it sometimes occurred that he went to
the Pardees for a pretended fourth time—the whole
route there: two miles to the town, one and a half
through it, and four round by the lake: all of it —
but only in his mind. Meanwhile, in Sand Spring
itself, people now and then tried to josh him about
the sisters as the two veterans had; a love affair in
such a place is often half audience. But as summer
came on, it happened as might be expected; people
forgot. Jim, on the other hand, though he didn't get
out there, found himself mentioning them now and
again; clearly he thought of the sisters as staying the

way they always were, suspended, if not actually waiting. And if this had no direct value to the sisters themselves, nevertheless, somewhere along the stations of life they had gone up a bit. In one way or another, for somebody, they had not passed out of mind.

And now — the mate. We haven't talked much of him or seen his side, though we will. Perhaps we had better do it now; that way we will at least know more about him than he did himself. As the intenser emotions go, the mate certainly wasn't a late starter, but he wasn't hard about them either; he was sudden. To judge him correctly, as he went at a woman with his bull forelock, this ought to be said. Jim was a more practical man; he let himself dream of love. But the mate was romantic, he wanted a wife. That is, now that a house and lot had come his way, or almost, he wanted children to staff it, and that's one way to do it. He was always on the hunt for reality. Of course, he thought of all this as practical. But if you're going to be hunting reality instead of submitting to it, it's best to be sure you're hunting all of it. What the mate actually wanted was to find himself at the prime of life a self-made man, and everything tidy. In Lancashire, as a blackish boy called "our Jim," he'd seen this kind of life or thought he had, as far above him as the bit of blue sky to be climbed toward from the bottom of the mine. In France he thought he'd glimpsed it too, pointing it out to Jim in farm after farm of the kilometered farmland, every last tended inch of it cantilevering slowly toward heaven — until laid waste. In America, he said, once a boy had arrived here, it was no longer necessary to look upward, only to wait to be of an age to work and to root as prescribed. For this country, now that it had untangled itself from its own notions of Hiawatha, was already up in that fine blue, with almost everybody here. He'd pointed *them* out to Jim also — the tidy possibles all around them — a whole hemisphere of the self-made. Jim, floating his own watery pastures, had nodded, unable to communicate more than a tinge of his transportational feelings, of all the crowds of barges and liveries going down, derry-down, one after the other, ever since the first ape got down off the first limb of time.

"*Down?*" said the mate, his eyes staring ahead even of his hair. "Not in our time. What else can you expect of course, if you get mixed up with horses? Or sail." He knew barges didn't sail in that sense of course, though it was a question whether he knew that earlier in their history he would have had a point about the horses which had pulled them; he was speaking generally, or so he supposed. "Not in our time," he repeated. "Not the way the wheel is going now."

They were just finishing off half a lemon meringue pie bought at the local Sand Spring bakery, and it was awful stuff; back there so early in the century it wasn't all good homestyle cooking, though at that period only a bachelor might know it. With his fork, he scraped absently at the hard pie-shell left on his plate, a sign of how bad it was, that even this lightning-careless eater had balked.

"Ought to be another bakery here," he muttered; this was early in their housekeeping together; after that, for dessert they ate fruit. *"Down?"* he said again, at the same time digging the flat of his fork so hard into the crust that the tines clanked on the plate and the gray, floured bits flew. He was always a violent-moving man, everywhere except in his work which was so delicate; well, you know him, you know. Then, as if he knew this, catching himself about to slap Jim on the shoulder, he carefully rested his hand there instead. "Not this kind of wheel, not in a hundred years, Jim. Why — " He smiled slowly enough, his eyes blind on that horned hair of his forever probing forward. "And the first hundred years is the hardest. "Why — " And then he had to slap Jim after all, his hand coming down even harder than first intended, so that even brawny Jim had to cry, "Whoa."

But the mate's cry outshouted him. "Wheels?" he cried. "Why, son-of-a-gun; they'll be *our* ladder!"

So this was the mate, who was at the time, as you know, a surveyor. Already he had measured half of New York State with the aid of his old Gunter chain, and day after day was increasing his score; how should he know that this land-knowledge of his, pendulum-tied to the ground though it was, was still not necessarily of the earth earthy? So, this was the man who, when the most important kiss of his life, the wedding-kiss, still tasted deeper of fritter than mouth, didn't think one thing more about it. And this was the man who, standing in a parlor not the minister's and with sponsors not really kin to the bride, but with enough of the proper feather-hats tremoring and already so willingly remembering, and the bride like a rose in her rose satin since it wasn't a formal wedding, the pointed bodice of her as small at the waist as anything in Sears — this was the man who immediately after that kiss could shout out (with what the hats and even some of the watch chains could only take for heartiness since otherwise what else would they make of it?) — this man could shout out, "*I can see my* GRANDCHILDREN *now!*"

But let's wait a bit on a wedding which — and you might guess why, if you didn't already know it — concerned more than the mate. Let us get back to that time, past spring, on into the hottest summer, and after countless trips, sailing trips one could just as soon call them, to Oriskany — when the mate looked up from his stewed peaches to say, "What's about this Lottie, you once said."

He saw that Jim began to tremble. "Why, *Jim*," he said. Around the house they always named each other quite naturally, not having any trouble knowing who was who. When out of the mate's presence, Jim always called him "my mate" — not having to identify either the mate or himself to others being one of the virtues of Sand Spring. Whereas out of Jim's company, the mate, as if to emphasize that Jim belonged in the town more than Jim himself dared imagine, or as if referring to his friend's two years of higher education, or perhaps merely to qualities of character or reflection which gave him precedence, always called him by name — Jim. On the rarest occasions, as in the case of bankers but not waitresses, the mate would mumble out his own last name, then Jim's very much more clearly. There too, as in all their later walks of life, though he might tease Jim for his style of reflection (the while his own style of impulse never gave him time to ask for advice much less take it) the mate always gave Jim a tender, courtly distinction — the way one might treat a man wiser than oneself, even stronger, whose head, though ready and hard enough for any fight which came at him, was, nevertheless, compared to the speaker's, short on horn.

"Why, Jim — " said the mate slowly, "I wouldn't want to cross you up in any — " Nor would he. On their nights out together he didn't ever. He didn't have enough vanity for it — though more vanity would have changed his life, if not saved it; nobody gets saved. It wasn't that he didn't see people; he saw all his targets well enough, from old Skinflint, to the land he wanted the way a woman wants velvet, to the women too. As he once told Jim, he saw them all sky-blue upward, that was the trouble, as if he was still down there looking up to where they were all crowded waiting for him up there in the clear, hard azure of that hole. What he never saw, not at the time, was the sight of himself going at them. He does now though; he's been seen to start out, then stop himself, many a time. And it helps him of course to know, as Jim knew way earlier, that though some nip and tuck is worse than others, nobody gets saved.

For right then, what shook Jim was another one of those glances at the future, which is all that philosophy ever is, isn't it? "What's about this Lottie," the mate had said. Jim coughed, to clear his voice. "I said 'Lottie and Emily,' didn't I?" he asked. "Surely I said 'Emily' too?"

The mate regarded him. Jim was never a target to him; maybe that's why the mate sometimes looked at him as if safety was there.

Jim saw that too — as the mate could always be sure of — but just now Jim himself was wondering. Had there been anything special in the way he'd said it, months ago? Or had it been in the way the mate had heard it — in which case, had it been with a hearkening toward something in Jim's manner or something strictly private to the mate? "Surely I said 'Emily' too," Jim said. "Didn't you hear it?"

Still the mate didn't quite answer. After a pause, he said, "Are we ever going out there, sometime?"

Whether they would or not, wasn't what had given Jim the shivers. It was — that if they did, things had already been settled, or else were being, now. It was — that right now, if the choice hadn't been settled on already, in secret archives somewhere — the choice was being made.

"Sometime," he managed to say, even nodding.

The mate nodded slowly back at him. "It was Lottie *I* heard," he said.

And this is the way things were in that part of the state when the last summer came for its interurban, overhead-track trolley cars. Here several explanations are in order, all of them swimming in the full, sad pleasure which is to be had in the description of any event single enough for its influence to be seen, yet faithful to an old cycle — and gone. We can let the cycle be for the nonce, having already said enough of barges and stables. But there still has to be explained how the main street of a town the size of Sand Spring, a street scarcely big enough for its own traffic light, came to be the terminus of a passenger carrier line which — though it never reached its plotted end a hundred miles away in the town of Batavia — did go along, neat as a parlor car on a leash, for twenty-nine of them, only to end up against a hillside in a gentle meadow as wide as a small lake, in among the rushes brimming the sides of an even smaller stream called the Little Otselica. To explain this will be an easy pleasure, follies of this sort being so familiar to everyone, and so acceptable when committed by the worldly — as this one was. Lastly, we have to speak in detail — some of it loving, but still so that you can see it and maybe even smell it — about the mechanism of that fine old sparkler and grinder, an electric traction trolley car. This won't be any harder, however, than you will someday find it to talk abour your old Thundereagle, or Hawkspit, or whatever it is you call those ruby-throated sports cars.

A Folly, says my dictionary, is a costly structure considered to have shown the builder to have been foolish. Add to this, that to my mind a folly is never really very national in outlook; men have been known to build castles-on-the-Rhine up the Hudson, and along the Colorado a Petit Trianon. Follies like these don't say much about the spirit of a country. Or much that's profound. But to my mind, a real, home-grown folly can be very local; I would know one of the upstate New York variety anywhere. On land, that is; what to say about the ones on wheels is still in question. But in any case — whether it's a castle standing dark against the vegetable green of an impossible mountain, or the friendliest tramline trying to sputter between mile after mile of people's herbaceous borders — what such a Folly shows is the spirit of the owner, just before that breaks through into humanity, or dies back into it. And humanity meanwhile being what it is, the kind of folly which delights *it* most is the hopeless expenditure of a man very well known not to have gotten his money the soft way, the whole history of his happenstance meanwhile being common knowledge round about home. On all scores, Adelbert Riefel's folly was of such a kind.

The Riefel house, running to pillars in the front, strange Amsterdam-style peaks in the servants' quarters behind, and two lions couchant before — and as such merely one of countless minor monuments to the last quarter of the last century — is still to be seen, and still appears to belong to a town larger than Sand Spring. Built on a fine central plot at the beginning of its owner's prime, always in heyday use in its carriage days, and later cut up into first-class apartments which never went unrented, it took care of him at the end of his prime, or what in some men would be past it, so that, except for what it harbored in its basement, the house itself was never a folly at all. Adelbert himself was the son of a scholarly Swedenborgian farmer — which belief we were taught in those days was part religion, part a sort of science — though that might be contested now. Adelbert, as far as anyone could see in the beginning, took over only the science part; like many another son of scholarly religionists, he went after money. First off, he went after a wife with it; he was a thinskinned redhead with a profile which must have taken on quite a nimbus at the courting hour, and indeed stood him well otherwise, all his life. Her money, it was said, was his stake. And the business he went for was fresh and decent enough: garden seed and related products, arboretums to hog-chows to fertilizers, but the rumor was that he was not benevolent. He was said to have taken advantage of all the financial panics of the eighteen-seventies except the last one, foreclosures sprouting an empire in his pockets. Mrs. Riefel sweetened the scent of their money by acquiring — at first not in the home house but in a conservatory in a rented one on New York's Fifth Avenue — one of the largest collections in the east of cattleyas, which she told the home garden club later was a *fancy* word for orchids. Then, at about the time of the last panic, though the Riefels were still unquestionably solid rich if no longer fancy, they came home to stay. People always wondered why, in Sand Spring this kind of change not being considered reason enough. Maybe the people Riefel'd grown used to taking advantage of out there had become his enemies — or his friends. He was still a young man, not even forty, younger than his wife. Maybe Swedenborg had bit him in the brain after all. Anyway, he came home.

Although Sand Spring social life wasn't of any level for them to lord over, give the Riefels credit, they now and then visited the cousins they had in town, and now and then had them formally back. According to them, he was as polite as all get out with them and with everybody, with the staff that served the house (a cook and a man from the "east," by which the cousins meant eastern New York of course) and with the rest of the neighborhood — he was even polite with his wife. According to these cousins, to whose social advantage if was of course to keep up the legend, anyone could see that formality was ingrained in Adelbert now. He had a library, so-called but also with books in it, in which he spent some time. His shirt collars sat out above his jackets in a way that none of those townsmen could match, even those who bought the best Rochester had to offer, and his cuffs were long. He was used to sitting in on committees and, it was suspected, champagne suppers, and though he didn't take much of anything himself, kept a small cellar for occasional visitors from the East and sometimes farther, though compared to western New York's groaning board his company dinners to anybody were very plain — the kind it took this sort of formality to be able to give.

Oh there were all sorts of details which would have been overlooked by anybody not as intelligently interested as the cousins — or the town. If he had the habit of light women, these were certainly not in the neighborhood, nor of course would they be; he would have mistresses, it was argued, whom he met in a hot, plush love-nest somewhere, though certain returned emigrés from the city (after all Sand Spring was less than four hundred miles away from it) said no, not that way, that it might very well be a much more rarefied business; in fact it might be what in smart circles was called not a love affair, but just "an affair." Certainly he went regularly to New York, though the manner of his goings and comings anywhere, if by nature distant with the town, was never furtive; now and then anybody could see him and often did, though even if the observer was only a foot of railway platform apart from him, and courteously spoken to as well, it still seemed to be from afar. He was at that time of his return a partially bald but still good-looking gentleman, who, if it was possible to compare him with his coevals about town (which it wasn't), already looked older than they did and yet younger; this latter characteristic was to emerge more and more. What we were looking at, I think, was a natural-born aristocracy, which the money had only added to — by keeping him in a certain state of organizational and philosophical health.

You've seen the type, we all have, and I've no doubt that the story of Adelbert Riefel, especially in those little details if not the big ones, has its place and specialty in the social rises of America at large, but we haven't got time for more of it than is strictly necessary, which some of it is. For remember the Riefel basement. In it there was already growing that engrossing folly whose later development, though it still didn't take up all of his time was to suck up almost all of his money, and would be of some concern to you also. For truly, in the furtive wheel-chain of life-events, those that can be picked out for sure as single and separate are very valuable. And it is a surety that without the folly that grew from Adelbert Riefel's basement, to become, as follies may for a time, a kind of practical enchantment — you grandchildren here and your daddies before you — all those unto the second and third generation that stem from Jim Eck and Jim Morgan, heretofore known as Jim and his mate, and in general to be known so hereafter — might not have been born. I'd go further, I'd say the odds are, in spite of occasional spurts of possibility (like that just now recounted mention of the Pardees) that you all would *not* have been born. And I ought to know.

Now — to the Folly itself. Your generation, I don't suppose it cares anything much yet for models or modelcraft that are not in the way of science or business — I mean model trains, boats, planes, collectors' soldiers, even model toy warfare. You're all for the hot-rod, or the stock-car race, or even the Saturday afternoon parachute jump at the county fair — for the moment, you're *in* it, as you like to say, for *real*. Chances are you don't know anything more about that other world than the Lionel trains I once got for all of you, all of them now in attics, or maybe

one or two balsa-and-rubberband airplane kits you
and some crony bought at a dime-store and put
together when you were thirteen. And I don't suppose your sisters know any more about it than their
old doll houses and tea-sets, or care — though there
are always some women who go on to those other
little pretties almost at once, to tiny furniture replicas of Williamsburg kept in a cabinet, or toy gardens
with Dutch bulbs in them the size of nailheads — or
even in their own lifesize houses, in not such an easy-
to-see, boiled-down way, though in the end maybe
nastier. Many childless couples have this fondness
for the wee also — wee dogs, wee talk — and the
Riefels were childless, but what fastened on Adelbert
was not for coyness or charm, and came over him
alone. It is a passion which can come over a grown
man — maybe one who's never had much of anything, or maybe a millionnaire in his maturity —
when either of them cries or sighs to himself "What
lack I now?" This is the way it begins, often — but
often there's more to it, much more. You can't see it
yet. Wait.

I understood it better, him *and* it, when, a middle-
aged man myself and down to New York on a business trip, I happened to go shopping for toy trains for
all of you children — grandchildren by marriage, and
grandchildren by right. It was after-war time again,
nineteen-forty-six, just after V-J Day — Victory-Japan,
in case you never heard of it — and countless wheels

[135]

we could all see had been turning like mad for
years, as well as the silent ones also, which we could
hear quite as well. But the little toy ones for the
moment had stopped. That big toy store on the
Plaza said that if the metal allowances were permitted they could still have what I wanted by
Christmas — this was only August — but I wouldn't
be there then, and they had nothing to show, to
order on. After they understood that the castles and
drawbridges, anything with soldiers foot or mounted,
didn't attract me these days no matter how medieval
— "We understand perfectly," said the salesman,
"we can scarcely wait for the *domestic* stuff, I mean
the peacetime, ourselves" — they gave me a list of
hobbyist shops where I might find secondhand
plenty of what I had in mind. I chose a shop on
Duane Street called the Train Center — trains, a
simple standard set of childhood ones, being all I
had in mind. This shop was out of business, I found,
but I found another on Park Row, and another on
Church. I had an afternoon to kill, and I killed it,
and meantime old Riefel, whom I'd seen that summer of nineteen-twenty, and whom I had things to
thank for, once more came alive.

You space-eater, you of the hot-rod — ever stand
in one of those concentrated essence places called a
hobby mart? Ever stand in a motoring headquarters
for planes, boats, cars, railroads, and miles of track
and roads for all of it, and miles of air too — which

isn't more than fifteen foot square? Only to find out
that people don't only buy them, they make them,
with dinky models and construction kits and a host
of suppliers and factors to this world — or they have
them made for them, nowadays everything from TT
trains to HO trains and roadways, to Frogkits and
Minic Ships? From there I wandered into a shop that
stocked ship-model supplies, blueprints and fittings,
woods and veneers, then on to a shop that made only
"experimental" models, by God, then to one which
only did repairs. I saw them all — and, out of sentiment let's say, I've even now and then kept up with
them, though not to buy. You of the Thunderbird,
ever hear of model-car racing? Slot-racing? With
equipment radio-controlled? But it was already all
there in essence back then, the world still hasn't
digressed that much, and it was then I understood
what you've got no cause to yet, and what Jim and
his mate didn't have any cause to understand either,
the afternoon that Adelbert Riefel let them see his
basement plan.

It's that after a certain age, and only after, there's
a certain pleasure in seeing the world once again in
miniature. Call these things hobbies if you wish, or if
they get larger, follies, but they're not of childhood,
nor of those akin to senility, and are never the
devotions of youth. As for seeing the world in small
but perfect, perfectly tidy, or having an urge to make
it so, that's as it may be; this is the passion the

partners thought they were witnessing that day. But I'm inclined to think otherwise. I think of it as a passion to see a world in small all right, but an enchanting and difficult one, a world with all its power lights always blinking on and off again, always in need of experimentation or repair. A world in small, all right — but for *real*. And I think of it as a reflective passion. Some of us, as you have good cause to know, take it out in talk. That's the commonest way. But Riefel had done it this other more solitary way, and perhaps even here had done it uniquely, for in shop after shop I saw nothing like he had, and maybe there never was. The urge to be unique in these affairs persists; maybe you remember what I came home with that year, the French-gauge electric train that no transformer could ever make really run? But Riefel's fault, and no doubt his reflections too of course, ran deeper. And — so did his folly. For in the end, he tried to see his world both in the small and in the large.

He must have had his small system custom-made, perhaps even in Europe, the cars and the whole thing, though that afternoon he didn't tell us this — the partners that is — saying only that he'd drawn the entire design and blueprints himself, taking the whole of one year to do it — the year he and his wife came back to Sand Spring. The execution of the plans had taken two years more. Maybe this explained the trips to New York, or maybe not — for

when the mate made his acquaintance forty-odd
years later (on a train connection out of Albany), he
was still going there. Mrs. Riefel had long since died;
her orchids had withered, replaced by housekeeper's
fern; the house had been cut into flats. In one way of
looking at it, he was only an old man of eighty-odd
living on the funds of a once-grand house and on
only one floor of it: did I say he retained just the
basement floor? But in another aspect he was marvelous, sharp as ever but quietly so, none of that
eighty-year chirp in him; in a ghostly way he was still
even redheaded — and going to New York. But perhaps, yes — though we couldn't know for sure of
course at our age — perhaps he wasn't quite so distant any more. Although it was the mate he'd first
met up with, he appeared to know about Jim; here
was the town again, at its function.

"I understand you two are mechanical in bent," he
said, shooting one of those cuffs. The cufflink in it, as
the mate described and Jim saw later, was as modern
as anything you might wear, but in those days was
still very advanced — an abstract design. "Perhaps
you'd like to take a look one of these days at my little
system," he added. He always referred to it that way,
to differentiate it from the big one. "Of course I can't
quite keep it up in the style to which it was accustomed, can't get the parts for it. But it's still worth a
look."

Worth a look! We knew (the town again) that this

was precisely what very few people did get; the cousins, in addition to knowing all the other nuances of his history, had continued to keep the town well informed. It all began, they said, back in his financial days, the peak of them, when he floated some debentures for such systems, or whatever it is that men like him floated. While men like Harriman and Frick had been doing it with the railroads, our Swedenborgian had sectioned out this little specialty of his own. Perhaps he'd even been the czar of it. Whether or not this had been true, the toy system we saw that afternoon was in commemoration of — or reflection on — a czar.

Though this was what impressed me most, and you may record still does — once inside, we had to stare first (though he certainly didn't make us) at the living-half of the basement. For though the entry door had been very natty in a way entirely new to us, we hadn't been prepared, even by gossip, for all the tricks of books and low shelves and high-hung pictures, and colors, and white spaces and black nudes, and — culture, I suppose it was — we now saw. I don't have to prepare any one of you; get married even here, you'll have it. It was merely certain parts of Paris and New York at the time, that we were staring at. Or nineteen-sixty-six, in Sand Spring. Only, this time we didn't feel any flicker of the future to make us tremble. Before it might have had a chance to, he opened the door to the other half of his establishment, and there we were, in his system or staring down at it, at his vast little world.

Did I say it was a trolley system? It was, of course, though it wasn't the one in *this* room which had ruined him. Though his story was all in trolleys (or as the bond issues said, tramways), the one we were looking at wasn't the one which had solidified him down from really gossamer rich, years before. That other system which *had* bankrupted him or nearly, over the period of fifteen years during which it had been built, brought up dead against a hill, but nevertheless run, and during a subsequent period of five in which he had paid back local investors who wouldn't have paid him in similar circumstances but whom he chose to call his creditors — religion again! — well, the two young men standing there didn't need to have that trolley system described to them, by cousins or anyone else. They had ridden it many a time, sometimes when it carried them near one of the few places it was near, or now and then, on a warm spell like this one, for the fun of it, with a girl. For Riefel, after his miniature was completed, had done what a fool always does, or a hero (he was Jim's and the mate's for a while): he had exaggerated. Intending to glorify man and country, but forgetting what small potatoes both were in that neighborhood, he had imposed his vision not just on a basement room, but on a region. The state hadn't helped, nor the public much either, but he had done it, whether for

Mrs. Riefel to smile at him over dinner for, after a hard day in the conservatory, or for him to show off to someone else (the prospectuses and finally the pictures maybe) on hot Sundays — did I say he always went there Sundays, summers and winters too? — in New York. Anyway, with his own money, he had gone and completed to the third stage an idea which had graduated from the stock exchange to a hobby, and should have stayed there. He had gone on to build his transport system not only for real, but to human scale.

The two young men gloated down on this other one; they shook their heads and shuffled, open-mouthed. The way they hungered (until it was seen that their interest was mechanical not reflectional) it might have been thought that they were old. Riefel smiled, watching not his system, but them. Unlike most owners of machinery, he seemed not to want particularly to be asked questions on it itself, but Jim and the mate were at liberty to examine it, which they did for a long time. When Riefel finally sat down, his cufflinks glittered and shook; this might have been all that was said between the three except that it was clear to the pair from the first that they had touched him in some way; they could only think it because they were a pair, for afterwards he sometimes called one of them Damon, the other Pythias, though never especially caring which name went with which. And it was plain that he wanted to give them something — not the system itself of course, which the whole town knew was willed to the Smithsonian — but something he must have known wouldn't be apparent to them for a long time. Well, he gave it, eventually — as most of us elders do. Meanwhile, that evening and others, the pair looked.

And now, if I describe a trolley transport system through their eyes, so that you can see it and maybe even smell it, it won't make any difference, will it, that we are describing that one, complete in that room, instead of the huge, lumbering one that used to be on the road going from town, outside? The two systems were meant to be exactly alike, and except for the fact that natural wear-and-tear was a lot easier to repair on the large one than on the smaller — ha, wouldn't think that at first, would you? — and except for one other difference, they were. But when all transport of this particular brand is gone into eternity, which should be any day now, what difference will it make to the sound and shape and smell of what I tell you, that the smaller one of Riefel's systems ran the full projected hundred miles (scale so many inches to the mile) all the way to Batavia, while the other ran only twenty-nine miles, scale a mile to a mile of course, to the Little Otselica, then jammed up against a hill? Won't you still have all the information you need for that last trolley ride we're coming to?

What the two young men saw first was the artifi-

cial landscape of course, the stations and car barns,
tunnels and bridges and aqueducts that any child's
railroad set, any rich child's might have. But, where
even then these would have been crude plaster-of-
Paris glaring with smeared oil-color, and the roadside trees made of that fuzzed green permanence
which is the exact opposite of chlorophyll, Riefel's
landscape which he had painted himself was most
vague and delicate for such a construction, running
to pale hillside curves and winks of mirror-water; the
green, when bent to be looked at, wasn't one color
but dotted, and the trees themselves, which from a
distance appeared to flourish, almost to wave, were
not trees. In this way, it was the cars and their tracks
which were made to stand out, those long cars, some
with a maroon stripe from stem to stern beneath
their windows, some with an Indian earth-brown
one, but all the cars of the original gamboge paint
worn now to the true trolley-yellow, and above all of
them, the electric cables in one long pattern ex-
tended, like a black stitch learned by a master cro-
cheter, and beneath the cars, in ess-shapes or flashing
stretches, the tiny curves of pure steel. That way, the
whole machinery of cars, tracks and cables, whether
resting in silence, or in full, rocking motion with
switches sparking and the incessant clang of the
trolley-bell, appeared to be situated in or moving
through the misty-moisty of early morning or dusk or
even dreamland — but the cars themselves and their

immediate paraphernalia stood out with the utter and clear concreteness of the real world. Only in one important matter Riefel hadn't done what was attempted by his other effort, the *Batavia–Sand Spring Interurban,* as the larger system was known. Here in the miniature one, there had been no attempt at passengers of any kind.

Here, the only passengers were the giant eye and arm of the owner (who needed to be organist, machinist, conductor, trafficman and Jupiter himself, all in one) and the equally giant, transported eyes of the audience. When the two young men had got through looking on, down and in, and even riding, which was the effect intended, Mr. Riefel allowed them to insert their great forefingers into the cars, to flip back and forth the caned seats, which reversed for the return journey just as in any system, and to touch and even take apart the dummy airbrake, handbrake and controller-box, which in each car were proper replicas down to their minutest inner parts — and even workable, had there only been provided hands of a size to guide. And here he stopped to give them a long lecture on the history of the "tram" or street-railway, British, American and Continental, from Liverpool, Edinburgh, the Potteries and Brixton, Vienna, Paris, Budapest, Nice, to New York and Washington, steam, cable and electric, step-rail and grooved rail, open conduit and overhead conductor — until he had brought them, a-clang and along from the old horse cars with the straight stairway, into the very presence of the single-deck, eight-wheeled, two-motored, center vestibule or transverse-seated, steel-tired, trolley car which any American of those years, in his rightful riding mind though surely not knowing as much as this about it (but even if he woke up to find himself seated in one in his pajamas), would certainly recognize.

The lecture, delivered by an expert lover, was the best the young men had ever heard on this subject, indeed the only one. Unfortunately, the times being always in every generation what they are, there is little need for us to quote here, other than to touch upon, for purposes of that later ride, some loving hints, tips and confidences on the subject of trolley riding, which we might never get anywhere else.

He talked for instance of the tiny rheostats inside the controller-box, of the shift from "series" to "shunt" which helped give the characteristic hitch to the grinding-along movement of these cars.

"The old cast-iron chilled wheels," he said. "You should have heard those."

He made them notice that, this being a country system, the roadbed wasn't paved, as required in cities, but laid only with a sett edging along each rail, the remainder of the surface being completed with tarred macadam, as could be done in country districts.

[146]

"This was also one of the economies we could put in on the Sand Spring–Batavia," he said, with a nod which, though neat, was the first old man's gesture they had noted in him.

Already they had noted for themselves that over and above the wheel-sounds, there was a constant play and obligato composed of the intermittent gush of the airbrake, the ting of the bell, the hard pull-up of the handbrake which at various points was required by rule to be tested, and wherever, by means of a movable switch, a car was deflected from one road to another — a zazzle of sparks. With a fine tongs, they themselves could turn clockwise the motorman's controller, though not grasp its wooden handle.

Finally Riefel, after advising them on the relative costs of conduit and overhead construction (the last being cheaper) ended with a little homily on design, pointing out that in the miniature system, as in the Sand Spring Interurban, the two overhead conductors were supported by ears from bracket arms carried on poles on one side of the road only, rather than by span wires strung across the roadway from poles on each side.

Now, all this time, both young men had been wanting to say something more than Oh and Ah, something to show their special comprehension, the way one wants to do when a man shows you the mechanical love of his heart. Accordingly, the mate seized this moment. He nodded. "That way the cables are much less of an eyesore."

From Riefel's eye on *him* — not cataracted wide, noble and frozen, the way an old duffer's eye should be, but still moving young and shifty — the pair knew at once that such words as eyesore were not remotely applicable to the system ever, not if poles had been strewn like matchsticks — or maple trees and telegraph poles — along the roadway here, or outside. But aristocracy has better reproofs, or folly has, both leaning heavily on superior information.

"Put it this way, gentlemen," said Riefel. "Dispensing with poles altogether is possible, and can improve the appearance of a *street*. If — all you *have* is a street." He touched a finger to the controls, lightly, but did not set them going.

"Where permission can be obtained," said Riefel, "span wires are sometimes strung from rosettes attached to the walls of houses on either side — of a *street*."

He paused, while footsteps were heard at the ashcans outside the rear wall of his estate, and a few seconds later, through the high small grilles that windowed the basement, the housekeeper's shoes went by. Already the visitors could see how uncalled for the mate's comment had been, even silly. Houses on the path of the system here, as on the Sand Spring–Batavia, were only occasional. They could see that this was not a village street but countryside, at times even open country, wild and imperial.

"But this is an *Interurban* system, gentlemen," their host continued. "Village-board ratifications, individual permissions? The object is to avoid all that, in favor of cheap, unoccupied land. The object, gentlemen, is *distance*."

He said all this in a twenty-by-forty basement room, but it didn't sound crazy, no more than it would once have done in a paneled room bank-high somewhere — or no more than other systems have, at other times. "That method," he continued. "The method of the rosettes?" He pursed his mouth as if they had mentioned these, not he, and as if, behind those words he was meanwhile ticking over whole manuals of methods he wouldn't bother their patience with. "This method has been largely adopted in *Germany*."

Given the times, the emphasis was perfect. They saw what a salesman he was, final proof being that, watching his manicured fingertip, they hungered for him to set the system all to going again, all the dream-miles of it, bells and switches, sparks and clang — but he didn't. Hungry they remained.

When they got out of there, they spoke of this, of what a salesman he was, and of what lessons he could teach them for use in their own business, though lessons of just what remained back too far in their minds to be fastened on precisely, or just on the

[149]

tips of their tongues. But curiously enough, the fact that they saw the folly too — could even ride out on it to Otselica, sitting in real seats — made no damn difference. As prospectors themselves, the sight of a folly like this could even make them tender, over another man's noble mistakes.

"Felt like a stockholder myself," said the mate. "A possible one." From his tone, it was an interesting feeling. "Open my mouth, I thought, and one of those debentures will float right in. Ho-*lee*, Jim. To own that sort of thing, not only land, but a whole — system."

"And did you notice, Jim" said Jim slyly, "he always referred to it as the *Sand Spring*–Batavia? Never, not once as people do, as the *Batavia*–Sand Spring."

After that, the two managed to go back fairly often, more often than not with some tribute token from their nimble fingers, maybe wire replacements, or hard-to-get parts for the motor-generator or static transformers; once Jim made a tiny battery with his own hands, and once the mate dealt with one of the bogies — that's a swiveling truck, you hot-rods — from the main body of one of the cars itself. They got used to the housekeeper coming in there, down to the basement, with a pitcher of grapejuice or lemonade, the pitcher being one of those huge, zinc-lined, silver Reed and Barton coolers which good houses in that part of the state and westward used to be sown with, and they got used to the sight of that dandified cufflink pouring it, neither of them missing the good whisky he must have known they never drank anyway. Beer, on the other hand, wouldn't have been proper to the relationship; from him, who never drank it, to them, it would have been almost an insult; these social distinctions, or menial ones, run very fine. Or used to. Meanwhile, if Adelbert Riefel had any champagne memories, these didn't appear to bother him, or else were spared for other environs; as for his two visitors, whatever the effect upon them of civilization — as I believe it is called — they were unaware of it. When the three of them bent over a section of track which was out of alignment, or examined an insulator, or touched up a chipped platform-finish with a bit of japanning, none of the party of three ever spoke of anything but what was immediate; nothing hots up the present better, does it, than a bit of mechanism to repair?

So, as that spring wore into summer and was finally lost there, and the basement system flourished — looking sprucer and running better, its owner said, than in the last thirty years of his tinkering — it came as almost a surprise to the two partners when, as August came forward, town chatter recalled to them that the terminal moment was drawing close, ever closer, for the Batavia–Sand Spring. For the Interurban, however one might choose to put the rest of its name, was dying, not at the usual rate, which had seemed to keep pace with general mortality, but speeded up now, as a transportational disease sometimes does, so that everyone can see its end coming. In this case, state bonds issued to underwrite the cost of a highway along that very roadbed had found no want of subscribers; at midnight on the thirty-first of August, the Interurban cars must stop forever, officially dead.

There are always some, however, who will make a celebration of anything, and indeed they may be wise. Not every turn of the wheel can be as clear as this one, at least to a certain section of the populace, at a certain time. Not every system dies, clean and elderly, in a field. Who celebrated the last phaeton, chariot, *growler* — yes, we'll come to that; who, for that matter, in that neighborhood and eastwards, the last ridden-for-need, non-racing horse? In this case, a full centennial not being in order, the event would take the simplest form and a very chaste one compared to some which have been heard of — in the shape of a last trolley ride — to the end, ride a cockhorse and back again — of the system itself. Whatever junketings and picnics always cluster around such affairs began at once to do so, but the men of the committee in charge, seeking for more dignity, suddenly found it. And in America, this kind of dignity means history, no matter of what kind. Mr. Riefel, follyist but founder too, must be invited, if not to preside over the fête, then to be present and honored in the character which thirty years had given him, as a "past pioneer." It was a question whether he knew of his own transformation, unconnected with the company as he had been since it had lost him his fortune; but in any case, such an invitation, to a man of his distances, was difficult to broach. The cousins, dead as his wife's orchids, could no longer advise. The housekeeper wasn't up to it. His tenants couldn't say they knew him well enough to ask him — who in the town did know him, more than a nod and a greet? But, as usual, Sand Spring had been watching. So, it was entirely natural, just as it was for the two Pardees to go on being forgotten in so many connections, for the two Jims to be remembered in this one. "Unless," said one of the committeemen, with a backward chug of memory which was for this town in no way remarkable, "unless — and of course it's no use to us — wasn't there once somebody in New York?"

If so, the two young men, as they walked toward the Riefel house one evening, bearing the town's invitation, handwritten by one of the librarians — knew nothing about it. Still, they were troubled to be carrying such an elegy with them, for so they considered it, on a night when they felt themselves so essentially alive.

The mate, whose hands were always cleaner than Jim's factory job allowed his to be, had the letter in a fist, but put it in a pocket as they approached the portico of the house. In the black-green dark, the big place with its several apartments all lighted looked solid enough, if not festival, and the porte-cochere still possible to carriages. Were they taking advantage of their friend, to bring such a request out of the blue, not an *up* blue, but fairly a down one, the mate wondered? Or, Jim wondered, was it an act of friendship to do it at all? And as was so often their custom, they wondered these things aloud. The Riefel lions, gloomy as usual, gave no hint. The basement door, ivory black and with a thin gold knocker, snooted them, but this was usual. There remained for Riefel himself to help them with what advice could be given — and it was Riefel who gave it. Their problem was merely to think over what it was he gave them — for forty years after, if necessary.

When he let them in they saw that he had his smoking-jacket on, as always when he had been working on the system, plus the foulard neckerchief which he wore when taking "infusions" for his "catarrh." If things went as usual, he would apologize politely for the latter, the only apology he was ever heard to make. Shortly he did so, and as per custom, took them into the other room where, stripping his cuffs, he prepared to entertain them with a brief display of one or other of the elaborately worked-out schedules in the system's repertoire. This was the moment, ordinarily, when either of the pair would

[154]

bring out whatever they invariably had for him. "Look here, this lightbulb I found, think it's small enough?" Jim might say, hauling out a pocketflash bulb that might just screw into a streetlight, or the mate would bring out a battery, the size of four sugar loaves, that he had made himself. Today they brought nothing, and he didn't wait for it.

Next, usually had come a moment when he offered them a choice of the schedule to be run off; you understand that in a run of a hundred miles, or even twenty-nine of them, and in thirty years, there could be a good many variations, mock breakdowns, accidents, full and partial runs, which could be evolved, a favorite run of the two partners being: *Let's see you run as far as Pell's bridge in sixteen minutes* (one minute of ours being five of the system's), *run into trouble* (the least being to have some foreign object strike the vertical gate of the lifeguard, the worst being to have a "passenger" struck by the axle-boxes of the rear bogie truck, when leaving the car), *then change cars and return.* Riefel didn't wait for a choice here either, but without preamble gave them the full hour program which they had seen only once before — that first time — in which all the powers of system, landscape and the hand at the helm of all of it were to the fullest vaudeville displayed. It ought to have brought down the house, as it had then, but this time they all sat silent. Then Riefel did something he'd never done before — made

[155]

a criticism. "One thing I've never been able to add to it," he said.

"What's that, Bert?" the mate said quickly — no *mister* or pulled forelock for him, for which Riefel, who always winced with pleasure at this style of address, may well have picked him up in the beginning.

And: "Maybe *we* — " said Jim.

But Riefel shook his head, tapping his fingertips to a rhythm, making and unmaking a finger cage. "Oh — I suppose I could burn some oil, make some sort of blower. But it's really not tenable. Nor should it be."

"What's that, Mr. Riefel," asked Jim. "What *is* it?"

He was turning his beautiful cuffs down again, and linking them. "Just the true trolley-smell," he said. "Just — the smell." He quirked at them, to show he shared their amusement, which however hadn't yet appeared. "Just as well," he added, linking the second cuff. "A line has to be drawn somewhere. Just as well." What with the unintentional rhyme, it sounded, curiously enough, like an elegy. Then he stood up.

"Boys," he said, though often he called them "gentlemen" — "You might as well hand over what you have for me." He even held out his hand toward the mate's pocket. It was the town again, though they never knew via which part of it. He had known about the letter all the time.

He read it in their presence, no excuses and no comment, only in his narrowed lips and raised nostril a glimpse of how once, when he had wanted to be, he could have been rude. It may even have been that he wanted them to see this, to see him too, in full vaudeville. But they hadn't the experience for it, to enlarge on any further suggestions or displays he might have given them — what did that pair know of tickertapes and board rooms? So, in the end he had to tell them his answer, straight out. "No, boys," he said. "No. But I'll give you an answer to take back with you."

He went to a typewriter which must always have been there but they had never before noted, under one of the nudes they so often had. To the town-committee's letter to him — handwritten in the best Spencerian for courtesy, he rattled off a reply at sixty words a minute — for modernity? Who knew, after all, what was this man's cultivation? He slipped the sheet into an envelope which he left unsealed, and handed it over, back to the mate. "Read it if you like," he said indifferently. Then he smiled, with that nimbus which might still have caught him a million, if not a woman, even then. "But not here."

They understood then that they were dismissed; though the pair acted so often in unison, each was still as sensitive a young man as any to be found acting on his own anywhere.

Jim spoke up this time, the mate after all having

[157]

had the letter to present. "Then, Mr. Riefel — " he said — it was curious how this "Mr. Riefel" sounded more intimate than the mate's "Bert" — "Then you're not — "

"Going?" said Riefel. He glanced down at the letter he had just answered. "A last trolley ride?" he said. "And a medal?" He looked down again, as if to check what hadn't been important enough to remember precisely, or else didn't cater to his brand of recall. "For a past pioneer?" At a jerk of his head, quickly gentled though he didn't smile again, the ascot fell back from his throat. He didn't look ruined any more than he looked eighty. The ruin, if anywhere, was in the minds that looked at him; it can be wondered if for lots of follyists it isn't the same.

"Oh no, gentlemen," he said. "That isn't for *me*."

He was telling us what the world is, for a man of risks — not that we heard him.

"No," he said, gentler with us than we had ever heard him. "No, you two go. It's for you." He gave us a searching look; it could even be said he bowed, to what he found. "Yes, you two go," he repeated. "It's for you."

Then the pair went out of there, never to see him again or thank him, or curse him, for what it took two weeks — and forty years after that — to understand.

Outside, the two walked along with Riefel's reply.

Should they read it, they asked each other; did he mean them to? From street lamp to street lamp they pondered, in separate silence, and aloud. In their ears that alternating voice echoed, offering them advice they couldn't see, calling them gentlemen, then boys.

"What did he mean!" The mate's voice was angry. "About the trolley doings. That it was for *us*."

Jim was silent. "I dreamed," he said then. He turned excitedly. "I just remembered. That he shot himself. Tomorrow morning."

They both saw him according to their joint experience, his chin at that certain ghastly angle, blood all over the olive-green foulard — which was a color quite suitable to combat — alone on a foreign field all his own.

"No," said the mate judiciously. "That's *your* dream."

They walked on. The mate reared up his forelock. "It's a cinch he doesn't see us the way the town does. Or only. Reason I always liked going there." There was an implication that they wouldn't go, again.

Jim thought it over a few paces. "He sees us," said Jim.

Finally, one of them — it doesn't matter which — opened the note and read it to the other. It contained absolutely nothing the librarian couldn't have read out in the children's reading-room — nothing beyond

a formal thanks and a formal refusal, saying that he
would always have an interest in transportation, but
expected not to be in town for the ceremonies.

"He just wanted to get us out of there," said the
mate disgustedly. But a few steps onward, he
stopped again. " 'No, gentlemen,' " he said, in a fal-
setto that certainly wasn't Riefel's. " 'No, that isn't for
me. It's for you.' " He turned to his companion. "You
suppose he meant we shouldn't go for the town; we
should get out of here?" He paused. "Or — Oriskany." They had spoken to Riefel of it. The mate
considered. Then he shrugged, drawing himself up
with a pomp that was a little growing on him; after
all, there has to be some answer to the terrors of the
world. "I suppose he only meant — we were young."

"And simple," said Jim. He looked down at the
note. "We did the wrong thing. That the town asked
us to do it isn't any excuse."

"They only wanted to honor him."

"For what? For being — passé?"

That was a word much in the newspapers, those
days.

"For being self-made, that's what."

Jim already knew the mate's aspirations, of course;
his own were harder to explain, though he had tried.
He wasn't sure he was a man for risks, though he
might be one for responsibilities. What worried him
uniquely was the thought of so many men returned
from the war with twenty-twenty vision, but still, if

they weren't careful, going to live it out in the dark, not knowing which of the two choices was happening to them. What he wanted — almost as good as a religion it would be, mate — was just to understand what happened to him, as he went along. Was that so enormous?

He tramped on awhile. "Maybe they don't know why either," he said. "Why they asked him."

"Who?"

"The town."

The mate trudged along, hands in pockets. "Passé, eh? Then why should those hijinks be for *us?*" He gave an angry laugh; how mystery always angered him! "What's he preaching?"

The pair mulled the rest of the way home without talking, like two apprentices leaving the house of a master who had never quite seen fit to declare openly the nature of the subject under study.

At their door, the mate gave a snort, then a swagger. "Sunday week, that junket is — You for going?"

"Why not?" said Jim. "Nobody's going to shoot himself over it in the morning."

Going up the stairs, the mate yawned and stretched. "Transportation interests, huh. Maybe we ought to sell him a car."

But a few days later, they learned what these interests had been. Riefel had sold the house, as the good income property it was, for a crackerjack sum (the town's phrase) only to reinvest it promptly in some crackpot scheme (its phrase also) for motor coaches to go down the very highway which was to supersede the Batavia–Sand Spring. The house-keeper was retiring on her annuity, only waiting for the new owners to take formal possession — and for the Smithsonian. As for the basement, except for the art work and the books, which Mr. Riefel had taken with him where he was going, the rest of the stuff there was left to her also. Apparently he had already everything else necessary where he was going — in New York.

"Sonufa gun," said Jim. "So *that's* what he was saying!"

"What — buses?" said the mate. "That was his interest, huh?" He wasn't stupid, only not reflec-tive — or unable to wait to be. And Jim, to give him credit, always understood this, just as the mate gave Jim credit for being such a thinking chap, if slow.

"O.K., buses, New York City, what does it matter. Can't you see what he was saying to us?" Jim had to walk twice around the table, he was so excited.

"What?" said the mate, much used to these dia-logues, which he thoroughly enjoyed. "What's the revelation?"

"I'll tell you what he was saying." Jim whipped a napkin from the table, folded it around his own neck, ascot-style, and raised his chin, Riefel-style. "*See my dust,*" he said. "That's what he was saying." Then he pulled the napkin off again, and sat down to his meal.

The mate made no reply for a bit, as often when he was stumped, or slowed. *See my dust.* It was a transportational interest all right; it could be the supreme one.

The two of them could see it underwriting — or overriding — all others, a little searing tail-light disappearing round the bend.

"Going away *permanently*," said the mate after a while. Such had been the message to the housekeeper. "At eighty." He shook his head, the prime of life not being connected in his mind, with age. "Old *men —* " he said.

That's a chorus for you. For *you*, hot-rods.

Old men, old men, old men. And young.

And so there we have it all now — the war, the town, the Pardees, Oriskany, and Riefel — and the two Jims. And all entirely natural.

We need only a ride on the Batavia line, to make it all clear.

III

PEOPLE came who wanted picnics. The August day at the start was one of those gray, limp ones which make bunting look weak, but the powerful trees of the region would have done this anyhow. Even at the edge of town, at the siding where the four long, striped cars waited, the trees were as thick as if only they held the year up; once past it, and the green billowing would go on for miles. Nobody minded that it wasn't a day when colors flew; a couple of the mothers were heard to say tranquilly that the children would be the quieter, for not having to match their doings to a broad sun.

"Local adage?" whispered the mate, digging Jim with his elbow. Usually, he never went at the town for any of its doings — as was sometimes Jim's privilege. For months at a time, the mate's very speech would be as Sand Springish as if he had been born there; in matters like these, his control, then and later, was scarcely to be believed. Today he looked marvelous, with life, if not top good looks. He had as

much as said so to the mirror himself, while shaving
with a razor stropped to a murder-edge and singing
over and over a little catch that Jim had never heard
him on before. Talcum was delicate on his jowl, and
he had on the tweed jacket he'd got in London on
their way home and had stored since, but the bow tie
he sometimes wore for the waitresses was supplanted
by a proper four-in-hand tie. Jim, though not as
rakishly clean, looked all right alongside; he was
never a dresser. He was a worrier though, or some
would call his bent by that name, and now he didn't
answer, scanning the crowd, his hands squirming a
bit in their pockets. Bunting had its own way of
theatering up a crowd, as if the parts to be played
were already evident; within its framing ribands and
below its fluttering pennants, grannies jostled what
used to be called sparking couples and drugstore
cowboys; family circles were storming the cars to set
up two seats facing one another, then tonguelashing
the juniors for slapping back the seats too roughly;
everybody looked distinctly himself as long as he
stayed away from the trees; the trees could do nothing just now but wait. A group of black-cloth no-
tables clung together, speeches in hand; the cere-
monial part of this jaunt would take place at Otselica, or so everybody supposed.

"All sorts here," said Jim, his eyes roving; then his
hands came out of their pockets, having found what
they were looking for. "I know what it is," he said,

[165]

smacking his thighs. "We forgot lunch." They hadn't forgotten to bring it; they hadn't made it. Domestic as they could be inside the house, outside it, like bachelors, they forgot.

"There'll be hawkers surely," said the mate comfortably. "Or the Women's Auxiliary, with a bang-up supper. Can't be bothered ourselves with aught of that, today." Jim had never heard him speak like this, British but not his own Lancashire, more like one of their comics. The mate's forelock went up, as he surveyed crowd, trees, women, men and children — the world. The small exclamation he made then might have been in his own woolly, boyhood dialect.

"What is it?" said Jim. For a moment he had half an idea that it was Riefel, here after all for his honoring. A charge of disappointment — as of a hero dropped — went over him. The mate saw it, and understood it too, and shook his head. "No, Jim. Going toward the rear car." He lowered his voice. "Am I right? Look there."

He was right of course, about the women if not the hawkers. A buzzing line of them, burdened with salad bowls, pitchers and the like, were climbing one after the other into the rear car, surely setting up a commissary there. But this wasn't what made the mate's hand clamp Jim's nape in a vise, forcing him to stare only one way. Tag at the end of the line, a procession of three straggled after. The two girls in front might have been any young pair, sisters or not,

[166]

one thin and striding, one full-blown — but the thin
one had a large wire strainer on top of her bundles,
and the rosy one held in her arms a cannonball pot.
The sun glinted through the trees now on this
strange armor, as the pair came shyly but steadily
forward. A boy with a handcart pushed after them.
The potbellied iron affair in the cart might have been
the sisters' catapult, trundled along to storm a town's
ramparts. It was too small to be Bismarck, but it was
a stove.

The mate came around from behind Jim and stood
in front of him, watching, and continued so all the
time the stove was being hauled up onto the platform of the car, though the girls had long since
disappeared inside. His hands crept to his tie and he
spoke thickly to the tip of it. "We'll eat, luv," he said.
"Ohh, we'll eat."

By the time the ten o'clock departure hour had
stretched on, in the way of outings, to eleven, the
mate had managed everything, Jim following behind. Inside the commissary car, a few tame hus-
bands and boys at their mothers' apron strings were
helping make things fast for the journey, and the
mate, quickly attaching himself and Jim, in short
order found himself at the head of the crew. The
day's plans were for a box-lunch on the way or there,
an evening supper at Otselica, for which the women
had brought everything from Sterno heaters to
wrapped ice, and a moonlit journey home; it was the

full-moon part of the month. There would be swimming, of the mild, foot-or-two-deep water which
mothers love, if the dryish Little Otselica would
cooperate, and opinions were that after such a moist
summer it would. For, just as it sometimes happens
with a certain dinner-party, a regatta, or any other
form of social endeavor which may or may not re-
volve around some science of human motion, every
portent for this day on the Batavia Line — even the
gradual gilding of the sun through the trees as the
cars waited there — foreshadowed success.

The rear car had been singled out because, unlike
the ordinary ones whose seats were arranged toast-
rack style from stem to stern, it had an open middle
section where two pew-style slatted wooden seats
faced one another, leaving a space between where
the picnic goods could be piled; Riefel had a car like
it in his system at home. Front and back of the
center, the seats were like the trolley-style anywhere,
made of that old yellow cane which wore forever —
or would have — and with a metal handle at the
aisle-side top corner of each, so that the seat might
be reversed for the return ride. In the last seat,
forward of the platform where the stove stood in
readiness for unloading again, the Pardee girls were
sitting. Both of them had a high color, whether from
pleasure at the committee's having remembered to
invite them, or over their own business initiative in
getting themselves here, who could say? Jim, for the

life of him, couldn't walk straight over; he didn't
even want to begin all that doubletalk again, but in
front of him the mate was working steadily toward
that end of the car, and might have made it first if a
sweet, Quakerish old lady-hen with a round eye,
tight skin and china teeth — I can see her yet —
hadn't stopped him for talk and then proclaimed —
"Why these poor boys have no lunch along!" In the
general banter — "Now just who were you counting
on?" — Jim found himself facing the girls. He'd only
got as far as a nod when the mate came up the rear,
close behind him. Jim turned — yes, that's how it
was, Jim turned — and the mate, coming abreast of
him, stopped short, and gave the two girls the once-
over. He meant to treat them as ladies, then and
later, but a little of the waitressy warmth came
through. Lottie had her plump little hand in the box-
lunch; perhaps that was why she raised her eyes full
wide, while Emily, for all her spirit, lowered hers.
The mate's eyes were on Emily, no doubt of it.

"You're not . . . Lottie?" he said.

She shook her head, smiling slightly, but her eyes
on Jim now, as if to inquire what story he'd been
handing his friend.

"Why no . . . she's Emily." Lottie had just swallowed, and now she laughed comfortably. *"I'm
. . . "* A few crumbs clung to her small, freshwater-
pearl teeth. And it was Lottie, the behindhand one,
who moved over easily and made room between her

and her sister for the two men. The two men looked at each other; for the space of a breath perhaps they gave each other the once-over. Then Jim, the behindhand one, slipped in front of the mate and sat down beside Emily, and the mate slipped in docilely after, next to Lottie — after all, he was only wanting a wife. Her dress wasn't lowcut, but that bust of hers made any dress seem so, and the mate, being the shorter man, would have the closer view of it. On his other side, Jim was floundering in that worst of doubletalk, when a woman isn't saying anything at all. He had a feeling that whatever he said would set the tone for everything ahead of him — maybe they all did; the feeling itself was acknowledgment that a moment of choice had passed forever by. When his remark came it was another of those nothings. "You got to town," he said.

At first, the picnic in itself wasn't too much for personality over and above what a hundred years of lemon tea, and chocolate cake for the ants to eat, has trodden into memory's communal ground. Even eating in a trolley car — or auto, or aeroplane; just *plane,* you boys say — doesn't much change the reflections common to eaters of the hard-boiled egg. But here, once everybody relaxed into the riding, which happens in any vehicle, then they had the novelty of an outing in one in which they had ridden unthinking on daily errand and jaunt; it was the way it would be if the New York subway should stop forever, and the populace have a day of picnic there. There were stops for comfort along the way, with much hopping on and off of children and one almost-left-behind nursing mother who ran out to flag the lead car just in time; at each stop everybody remarked how well the committee had done its work, in even going ahead yesterday to Otselica, to set up facilities there. Everybody also reminded everybody else that the route was now being observed for the last, the very last, time, since when traversed again, it would be dark.

So far, there hadn't been any wonders of the world, only the two bordering townlets where they had stopped off, separated by a country road; for most, this was as far out on the Batavia line as any had ever been. But as soon as they had left behind these two hamlets, the leafage and the gradual wildness began; soon they were running along handily through a lovely vale, between arching trees which now and then met and tangled high above. It was a tingling pleasure to feel lost this way, probing a limited unknown, with the car grinding and swaying along its high wire, between one's legs that secret teasing of the motion, and all around one the caravan's sense of good provisions hard by one, and homely friends. There were no houses here to hold the span wires between them as in Germany; this was unoccupied land. The little boys aboard made a game of counting the poles.

The air grew cooler, delicious with vines, and those who had brought sweaters were wondering whether they should be the first to fuss themselves into them, when — the lead car stopped, with a lurch that sent people and packages against one another, but nothing broken, just one little boy down in the aisle. The news came relayed back, after an ominous quiet of precisely two and a half minutes; there was a jam in the overhead wires due to over-growth not having been pruned — nothing was wrong with the current however, all would duly be well. And in a few minutes, with a crackle from above, and a sizzle of the sparks the children complained were so hard to see in the daytime, they were off — a picnic scare, a picnic adventure, precisely to scale.

This happened untold times before the morning was over. It was impossible not to feel better acquainted all-round, characters emerging ever stronger, naming themselves from the settled corners of the car: the lady and children in seat Left Two, the couple up ahead with the big basket, the little Quaker hen forever nodding, the motorman up ahead, whom all were shy of speaking to, because he was to lose his job. The sagest heads of all nodded over the line's demise; clearly it had been the costly upkeep which had done it; no, said others, not with patronage it wouldn't have; it was because the line didn't go anywhere. "Twenty-nine miles to nowhere!" somebody said. "Unfinished, if it had been *finished —* " said another. Whose fault was that? Nobody was heard to mention Riefel by name in any connection, but several spoke of the buses to come, most with contempt; where cars as handsome as the one they were on had failed because people simply wouldn't, didn't, how would buses — and on a road-bed as wild and unpopulated as this? They were drawing along now, for once uninterruptedly, through the last few miles before the terminus; some wag had put up a sign which said "Shin Hollow," and a little farther on "Great Bear Mountain," which was in fact the name of the hill. Now the car swayed and ground on through darkest woodland; the com-mittee had had a man on the tracks clearing for a week before the excursion — buses *here?* Nobody could visualize it. Then the motorman spoke up, nasally proud; indeed he had been promised a job with the new buses, which however were going an-other route, and everybody was relieved for him yet irritated, since if he had been listening why couldn't he have volunteered this information earlier? Con-versation on this point all but stopped; appetites had started. A few voices persisted, halfhearted, on the subject of progress; consider how their own town had grown; since when had so many people in it barely known each other's names, as some here? Since the *war.*

The children meanwhile, hearing all this above

their heads, looked wise without knowing it; something new was going to be added to the life ahead of them; they were on the voyage they had all along known they were, the original voyage, *out*. Box-lunches opened everywhere, decided on quicker than sweaters, and with food, the talk swung round again to character; there were those two boys down in back to be kidded, the ones without lunch. But they're provided for — "Watch it, you boys." Livery stable, a voice remembered. Boys? They're men, those two boys. "Veterans," whispered someone, and character sank again before this most remembering word. "It's the last time," mothers said to children who already had the look of those who had been kissed by governors of the state, and would grow up to shake the hand of some President. Remember it. It'll be different, it'll be dark — going back.

The Little Otselica. The creek and the hill. At about two o'clock in the afternoon they reached it, that perfected moment on trolleybed, roadbed or airstrip — the *stop*. There, broadside of the road, was the big bear of a hill which had provided the bygone stockholders an excuse to desert and curtail (though in Riefel's home system it was tunneled through), against Riefel's professional counsel that a transportation system cannot curtail, none of them can, being wars against nature; like wars, they must grow or fail. But now, the central carbarn, from whose peaked weathercock a flag had been lifted, and all the other outbuildings, all built of good stone, trellised and guttered in that homelike style in which small provincial railroad stations and their ilk used to be, stood out against the hillside like a village whose inhabitants, piped away by some pied spell and now released, were thronging back. The committee went first, in their black garb rather like a funeral it was true, but right behind them the women came marveling, gingering up everybody's spirits, including their own, with their polkadots and kangaroo-pockets full of children; the spirit of picnics, and cemetery visits, is always feminine. Certainly there was reason to marvel; from comfort stations to water fountains, to stalls, tables and even a dais in the "main hall" of the carbarn, the whole effect was that of a village built for one day. Even the creek had come up to snatch, with a three-and-a-half-foot depth of water, just enough for a child's scream to convince its mother it was drowning. Only the stationmaster's dried garden, lacking a resident these two years past, could not be revived. In the office behind it, the committeemen retired at once to huddle over their speeches, thus at once creating a government and a populace — everybody else could go free.

The two buddies and the two sisters could now devote themselves seriously, in a circle on the grass, to the eating which had begun, at Lottie's insistent offers, in the car, and now advanced from mere

sandwiches to a spread that required damask nap-
kins and got them; where other women reached the
heights via cold chickenlegs, the Pardees' hamper, an
affair which ran to real cutlery and continuous magic
disclosure, opened on a capon still warm in its juices,
and a creamy oyster pie. Thanks to Lottie's prove-
nance — for though she quoted no recipes, gave
no sign other than the loving way she patted the
cloth like bedlinen and cradled the food in its
napery, surely the feast was her doing — there was
enough for everyone, except perhaps Lottie herself.
But on this one afternoon perhaps she didn't mind;
what she clearly asked of any hour was to be able to
nibble it away in company under the perfect excuse
of such an occasion; if the two bachelors had had
any early squeamishness about "accepting" it was
eased, in watching oysters go down Lottie's throat as
if to their duty, and that posy mouth redden, as if
with rouge. She was a dainty eater always, and
also — if the flow of food and the prospect was
constant — could acquire a kind of conversation. Articles were often read by her, as she ate alone sometimes, at home; did they chance to know that some
cows in Japan were kept in stalls, fed beer, even
massaged, to make the most succulent beef in the
world? She didn't know but that she'd almost be
willing to be a cow, in Japan.

"Wouldn't mind eating you," said the mate, lowering his eyes, but if Lottie heard him, as she dabbed

after a crumb lost just where his glance was, his gruffness was so solemn that it couldn't be rude. The mate, who in the car had once or twice studied Emily, perhaps to make certain whether or not those dark brows did meet or could, never glanced at her now.

And what of Emily, stuffing herself like the rest, who looked anywhere she liked — at the day, the crowd, the mate and Jim almost impartially, though perhaps not much at Lottie — occasionally raising a lazy, drugged arm from where she was lying full-length on the grass in a dress that matched it, and who now, her brows knitting once and then smooth again, leaped to her feet in one movement, as if clasping a trestle let down from the sky, and said in that caroling voice of hers — "I shall swim!"? Disappearing, she returned in the same heavy blue bathing dress, sleeved and bloomered, darkening to black in the water, that others already in were wearing, but she carried no boudoir-cap of the kind that were here and there ruffling the Otselica, nor the canvas shoes which laced most ankles — her feet were bare. She swam face down, with a boy's stroke, her piled hair sailing the water. Jim and the mate, having brought no suits, watched her from the shore. Though the stream was only a few yards wide, when she rose, billowing in that blue-black drapery, and started for shore, she seemed to be walking toward them from a distance, and when she called out something they didn't catch it; even when Emily spoke normally, it was always the silence Emily spoke from which one heard. A few feet away from them she stopped, the water draining down her legs, and tossed her head at them. If they could have eaten her, the taste would have been like venison.

And so all that day, as in the night to come, events dispensed themselves in the mists of natural action. In front of the hill, as twilight came on, the rounded carbarn, grouped with its flat-roofed outbuildings, glimmered like a natural farm. But then, when it came time for supper, and with the others the four entered the huge "hall" which only the committee's helpers had glimpsed, the two men stood back, in rank silence. Stalls had been set up all along the great length of the pounded dirt floor, and among these they caught sight of the girls' stove — but that wasn't why. Instinctively, both men looked up, expecting to see a few chinks of sky, but here in this place the overarching girders were securely roofed. And unlike that other place where the two had met, there were rails here, domestic to the ground, of the same kind that in the center of town made a bicycle skid on its way down the avenue. If the trolley cars themselves hadn't been removed from here, any resemblance might never — the mate spoke first.

"Is the hangar, our Jim, isna it?" he said. "Is the hangar, for fair."

One could smell the oily rags; for certain there was

[178]

that smell here; the crowd's hubba-bubba dwindled
to the sound of men — mechanics, pilots, ground-
crews. There was missing only the latticed sky, dirty
or shining like a mussel-shell, beneath which he and
the mate had worked their rags and told each other
of barges and blue glare at the top of mine-holes; all
that was missing was the down-whanging whine that
sent them for the ditch and the brave, incoming putt-
putt that stood them up to squint — planes didn't
sound like artillery shells in those days. As if all the
shell shock had been waiting there, Jim's ears filled
with these now.

They all saw how white he was, the mate said
later.

Emily spoke quick, reaching out her hand. She
was back in her sailordress with its middy-tie, her
hair damp-dry. "Come along, Jim, and help me." She
took his limp hand in hers. "Come along and help."

He went along, but as it came out to the mate in
bits later, for some hours it was to Jim as if the war
had come down and in upon him like a plane itself
— "like a plane landing through the roof onto the
dining-room table, mate" — it was the war-thrust, at
last becoming real to him, through no longer being
so. Which was the realer then, was it daily life, for
all except the dead on plaques? Could it be? Nobody
in the hubba-bubba here in the hall, even the lamed
or the bereaved, was thinking of the war in the
overmastering way it ought to be thought of — held

like a major wound in the mind. For some hours, he must have tried. Of all the remaining hours, through the din of supper, until he found himself with the others being loaded into cars for the ride back — he remembers nothing else.

"But it would take a Christ to do it," he told the mate later, and they both recall that they even solemnly discussed whether this was a reason for them to take harder to religion or give it up altogether. For you must understand that many of these bits being pieced together for you here and now, came out during a lifetime of friendship, and relationship too; half the time even you young fry don't stop to think which of the two Jims' grandchildren you really are. What if the main and most of what happened that day didn't come out in words between those two until a cold winter's day forty years later, when one said to the other, "Want to drive along and look at something; got something to show you, Jim," and two old men sat talking together, nonstop except to ease themselves once or twice, against a hill? The trip back, the ride back; that's when things really happen, even in memory. Though — even if nothing so secret had ever come out in such plain words before — all those forty years, both of them knew.

"Emily sat you down in a chair next to the fritter-stall," the mate said — that much later. "She managed you. You were cashier. Can't believe you don't remember, even *now?* And I was the barker, why I yelled myself purple, we must have sold more of those things that evening than the girls had sold in a year. Funny how, though I'm not much any more for even the best bread and cake — always begging your and Emily's pardon, and knowing what you've done with them — I can taste those crazy little snippets now."

"Recipe's lost," said Jim. "She always said."

"Sure is," said the mate.

And after a while and some further conversation, the two old men got up, brushed the loam from their trousers, got in the mate's Cadillac, and drove off.

But back to that day much earlier, when, after the commissary car had been reloaded, the two men and two girls left all that gear to the old hens who preferred to stay with it in the rear car, and made for the front one. As they climbed into the best seat of all, the last ones of each row, next to the back platform — where they could sit two by two and across the aisle from each other, the mate clapped Jim's shoulder hard.

"She bowl you over?" he whispered. "Or was it the heat?"

(Have I said it was getting sultrier and sultrier?)

Jim didn't answer, except with his shoulder, which took the blow unmoving.

"He's all right," said the mate out loud to all and sundry. "We knew you were O.K., Jim. Once you started making change."

And so he was O.K., for forty years, but still, those forty years later, going back in the Cadillac, and still being of the sort he is, and not too much shakier, he asked the old mate, " — and do *you* remember what you came up close over my shoulder and said to me while I was making change? Now I *remember*. About Lottie?"

"Yes, I remember it," answered the old mate, his voice final. And neither of them said another word about it, all the rest of the way home. Some things even memory is too late for, once they come out all of a piece. But we both remember it now. The crowd was full of faces; the body-heat in the carbarn, and the storm coloring the air sullen, made them appear mazy and on fire all at the same time. Behind in the stall the girls were busy but not forgotten, the one sister who was heard loudest in her silences and the other who was only something to see, but so much of it. The mate's hand was hard on the shoulder, the shoulder steady. "She's as solid a woman as anybody would want to stand by him. She's a dream."

"You mean — *her* . . ." said Jim.

"You know who I mean," said the mate.

Then, at least in that part of the world and its wars, it was time for the last trolley ride.

Lottie even said it out loud, in the tone of one who reads articles. "It's the last of the old Batavia. We must remember it."

"Remember what old Bert said?" said the mate —

who was now sitting next to her — to Jim. "He never could get it, the true trolley smell."

Think he never notices — that's what people often think of the mate. And then, months after, or forty years on — out with it. Anyway, it was the last anybody there spoke of Riefel.

And now to the night. Will you be shocked at the story from now on, and if so, *which part of it?* That's what I'm wondering. But even if we held hands in a circle, a seance, and tried, your generation could never tell us; you're not shockable yet, you think; you wouldn't know. And now to that night.

All the time they had been loading, that sulphur-green quiet before a summer storm had been building, so that children cried out, peevish against the invisible weight in their breasts. The night grew glassier. Outside the waiting line of cars — a whole arkful, racked up tidy with their bundles — the moon was high over the hilltop, struggling with a barrage of clouds. *A ring around it last night* — clustered up in all the front seats, as old women do, the hens were telling over the almanac of their bones. The head motorman, their cossetted pet whom they had fed and nagged and now looked up to trustfully, up in front with his back to them, now suddenly got down again, and was anxiously observed in consultation with the other two drivers. Meanwhile, in the car at first so welcomedly anonymous to the two men and the two girls, character

[183]

once more began willy-nilly to surface to the faces
and to peer from unexpected corners: veterans, librarians, other stall-keepers met tonight. In answer,
their own town faces surfaced, and they sat with
their eyes lowered: the two buddies, and the two
Pardees. Nobody spoke. In the yellow gloom of the
trolley car, it was the familiar moment, the one
before take-off, before — lurch and away! — the
gathering clop-clop of the post chaise. The motorman climbed back in, and waited. Then thunder was
heard, bringing the hills in closer, as it does in these
parts. Then they were all lively at the windows,
pulling them down as the storm broke, and the spell
with it, or so it at first seemed. Inside the sealed car,
while the rain swept white over the windows, the
chatter softened almost to dove-talk, the tender, fra-
ternal talk of the safe. Then it was over, and — they
had started! Who had noticed it, the spark and the
start, except maybe a child? What a success even the
storm had been! It was a real cloudburst, the hens
said.

Then they were swaying through the trees again.
For the party in the rear, the spell had just begun.

The trees were a dark aisle of plumes now, as if
the train of four trolley cars was running a gauntlet
which never closed in. The trees held the night up
for them, out to them, and there was only twenty-
nine miles of it — unbearable not to crush it around
someone and to one's breast. A waitress would not

have been safe here. How locked and stoppered all
their mouths were, in the moonlight that leafed their
faces, through open windows that poured their first
ride together back at them, cool summer balm. There
was a zest in the air no sweater could slake, only
arms. If the silence went on like this, or back into
chatter, this ride would be their last anywhere; all
felt sure of it but could do nothing. Only twenty-
nine, eight, seven — back to autumn, to Oriskany —
and out of mind. At what mile of it the current in the
overhead wire went out — and stayed that way for
two hours by hen-watches — I wouldn't be able to
say. But I shall be able to describe it to the inch, to
the nerve, as a man's tongue does, touching it. If you
laugh at it, I'll smile with you; if you shock at the
wrong moment of this account, I'll slap your faces.

Well . . . a few motormen's lamps were lit, of
course, one glassed-in red oil-glow to a car, just the
right light for the old to nod by, or the mothers to
cradle their lot with a *put your head down,* but
nothing to what the moon did for all the other
restless ones. Two by two or in bunches, all the
young folk, except for two pair of them, slipped to
the back of the platform, then down. All had to pass
the two men and two girls sitting in the seats chosen
as the most anonymous, the best. As the others went
by they would see the mate and Lottie stiffly figured
in the lurid light, her bust, his forelock. Across from
them, the other sister and the buddy sat rigid too,

but like those garden statues which have the beginning of a stone smile. And after a while, if any hen was watching, she could have seen only the one pair, in the red light still unclasped. Opposite them, that other pair had gone.

Just outside the car, the trees flung themselves in dark fountains, like Versailles. Then came a meadow, shimmering like parkland and as vast, then more trees. Through the window, and a round break in the trees like the bright end of a kaleidoscope, the mate watched that other couple disappear until they were gone. Though their story might take years to be made into words, as he sat there beside Lottie he knew it already, and forever.

Out there, where it looked so mysterious — "Oh it was," said Jim forty years later, "and I don't mind telling you of it; indeed don't we almost *have* to, now?" — out there, Jim walked along beside Emily, slow through the wet grasses and in rhythm too, though they had not yet touched even hands. A paragraph from one of Riefel's manuals, he said, kept blotting in and out across his sight — "For simplicity of operation the overhead system is best . . . supply of power is not interfered with by heavy rains or snow . . . duplicate conductors are used and repairs rapidly executed." He hadn't known until now that he learned things so profoundly, and wondered that she couldn't hear these words *duplicate, execute* attached like a hissing refrain to his steps.

[186]

Then he thought of what the motorman here had called out: "Take two hours at the outside to fix things, two and a half at the outside; things are that wet!" — and exulting life over miniatures, he laughed aloud on that black air — and was heard.

It was silver air that the mate saw, though he could no longer see them.

But under the trees, the air was surely black, in a patent-leather night with a gloss whose source could no longer be seen, and the ground was dry. Jim saw his own coat, miraculous on the ground, and couldn't remember laying it there. Then it was the moment that the locusts stopped, and in that buzzing silence, he thought he remembered everything else.

He could see the barge-canal, the lock bearded with green at the waterline, then the pocked brick and the flower-stuck crannies of the sides — if the barge was coming up in the lock — or the waving weeds on the lock's broad lip, even under the cross-beam of the gate, if the barge was sinking down. He could see the linkage, like an overhead wire or an underwater length of line, between trolleys and barges, though what it meant he couldn't say, or why it was a woman, the frittering women, who made him see it; she and this were fathoms deep. The war names came on now as never before and tumbled through his kisses, from Verdun to Chateau-Thierry, all the great plaque-names he had never been at, down at the bottom the faintest script of those he had — and all telling him what up to now he had avoided: that it was his lot, his common lot to have to choose between terror and charm in all the moments of life past and to come — either to remember blood and death, to rise on their crests toward acts of atonement and change he knew he was not capable of — or to sink, sink, in the arms of the daily, under the daily charm. He remembered the washlines of that spring, and their mystery; what was the message of daily life, of a profundity that never stopped?

As he wrestled there, the town came and stood at his side, almost as if it needed to have people break out and away from its conversations — even lived by it. By how much or how often a man himself broke out of it, was that how his life was made?

And all the time, there was Emily hot as roses under him, learnèd in all that Europe hadn't taught him, or virginally born to it. She made him feel as if she was on the barge — a figurehead of those lost certainties — and he was on the land. The doubletalk that belonged to life was inside her. He reached it. She played him up and down like a ball on a fountain, and all the time, he saw the seriousness of her eyes.

When they came back to where the four cars were still lined up on the track, with the electric lights on again inside, they managed to attach themselves to a noisy young group just coming out of the woods from another direction, their trumped-up catcalls and banter fake even to themselves. "Why —" he whispered to Emily, doing it for the intimacy — "the woods are full of us." Looking back, he whispered to her, "Anyway, we've left the town there." He was bold enough to say so, if somewhat darkly, to the mate, not a week later, when certain preparations were already in order. Whatever Emily thought, they had stepped back into the car just then, and she had turned majestic, her cotton dress somehow straight as tin again; that he had slipped beneath it surely no one would believe. Nothing showed on him he felt sure, not even to his friend. When things go so right, a man's flesh — and I suppose a woman's — feels calm and even, doesn't it? Only the mind, mindless to its roots, is drenched.

The interior of their car, left in the pall of one red lamp, had changed. Now that the current was back on, it was bathed in yellow light reflected from all that varnished wood and cane, portaled by the in-pressing dark. In other ways too, it was like a picture. The mate and Lottie were the center of it. They hadn't changed their seat, instead seemed to have grown there, with big hamper and box beside them, or was it that the balance of the car — old wives and young, widows and a few men either old or woman-humbled — had turned to or gathered round them? The mate glanced up once as the others trooped in; he was talking. All were listening to him. Lottie's eyes were gleaming, and her fresh mouth too; though candy was circulating from a big goldpaper box beside her, no one would know she ever ate the stuff, except for the heap of candypapers in her lap, between her demurely draped knees. The mate had been telling them what people ate and drank in the county of Lancashire where he was a boy, such talk being a way to the hearts of many, as well to one. He had been discoursing for some time.

"They'll offer you tea, luv," he was saying — to everybody, or to one. "And they'll offer you what they call 'ornaments' with it. 'Ornaments, luv?' they'll say." His voice was charming, self-charming. "And what'll they mean by this?" He roared it.

Just then, Emily and Jim sat down in the seat across the aisle, and they and the others who were trickling in, immediately they were seated, turned round to watch him.

"What'll they mean?" he asked in a smaller voice, like an actor. He flicked one glance at the pair in the opposite seat, then did not look at them again. "Why — " he said, in the big voice " — why, they'll mean whisky, or rum!" He turned to Lottie. Sitting down next one another, their eyes were just even, he being short legged but long waisted, her waist being where one could not quite tell. "That's what they'll say, luv," he said to her, and for her only. " 'Will you have ornaments?' "

But if nobody therefore looked at Jim or Emily, or

seemed to search for other miscreants, this didn't mean nobody knew, or wasn't going to gossip about such walks in the woods, later. If they let it go for now, this was because another morsel had been handed them, more tangible, and — wrapped in candypaper as it was — more palatable. This way the town could claim itself audience only to what happened in ways which were seemly. This way, the proprieties were kept — and the mate and Lottie were assisted by them. And no one at that time, not even Jim and Emily, took their need of such assistance as a sign. For in the sight of all, as is said in the marriage service — in the golden, interior light of half-past ten of an August voyage, in that arkful of people, idly waiting among the crumbs and the children sleeping like pigeons, waiting to ride home again — as well as to endorse, countenance and recall by date any and all contracts or other engagements entered upon during said voyage — in the sight of all, Lottie and the mate were holding hands.

As the motormen signaled one to the other, and the train of cars was off again, this time to ride silkily all the way home, the mate stretched an arm straight across the back of their seat, but the hand dangling on her shoulder, and began singing. He had a light baritone voice, sweet enough to be a tenor's had he been Irish, and he was singing the catch he'd begun the morning with.

"Four *arms,* two necks, one *wreathing,*" he sang, "Four lips, two hearts, one *breathing;* fa *la*-a-*ah,* fa la-a-ah, fa la la la la la *la!*"

Through all the bypasses of the night, the whippoorwill starts, and once a stop and an owl-call, as we went banging through the countryside, he sang it. "Four lips that mul-ti-*ply,* all in-ter-change-*a*-bly!" and after a while some in the car answered him: "Fa *la*-ah-a, fa la-ah-a, fa la la la la la *la!*" There was the special smell; combined with the clinging odor of fritters, it made a perfume they knew they were never going to smell again. The lights were out again now, but only for the babies' sakes; the motorman's searchlight, cast on the tracks, seemed the other end of a glowworm — a trolley car is long. Deep in its well somewhere, a voice called out, "This is the life!" and another answered, "This *is* life," and a third one said, "Oh, razzmatazz," and none was identified — who speaks in his own voice? But everybody knew what was meant; we were just as smart in those days — in our Greek-revival farmhouses, which we didn't even know bore the name — and before, back to the days of Greeks a-riding the Aegean, in what was probably called the last trireme. People have that kind of dull knowledge built in the bones by time; it's only poetry and uncomfortable when they mention it. Or song. So they rode on, and at last came the solemn forever, the stop. It was the last time, the last in life or eternity, and each leaned back in his seat with the pleasure of one who had survived even that. People make these solemn ceremonies for themselves of course, just the way they have to cast back and cast back over an event of love, to help remember they've had it.

Short of weddings not one's own, somebody said — or funerals ditto, somebody added — all were agreed it was a perfect experience. And so, Jim and the mate named Jim and the sisters Pardee had their audience, captive to them as they were captive to it, and this was the way, with a fa and a la, two and two made four.

Weddings are supposed to be all the same, it being the long, long road winding away from them that counts. We ought to describe these two nevertheless, leaving you, the fruit of them, to judge.

Lottie, as the elder, was to be married first — "Did you know she was older, Jim?" asked the mate, and when Jim nodded slowly, the mate came back with: "Oh, not that it matters, I've still got the edge on her; it's only that sometimes, it's hard to believe." He was leaning in his old place for talk, in the dining-room archway of the little house they shared, and he looked less burly than usual; the worries of approaching matrimony had scored dark circles under his eyes.

"Emily does — look older," said Jim carefully. During these intervening weeks, though confidences

[193]

had come to a standstill for the moment, in a queer way this had further ripened the friendship; since the old, dangerous nights in French territory, they hadn't been so tender and sparing of each other's feelings and needs.

"Ah — it's not looks." The mate spoke judiciously also, now that each was speaking of his partner's choice. "That's a wonderful girl you've got there."

"There's no one like her," said Jim with a deep laugh he couldn't help; he was stunned by her, enthralled. He and she were meeting daily in all the places that were open to rural lovers, building themselves the kind of private legend that never hurts a marriage; he had climbed out of her window; they had slept naked in leaves. Often he had climbed in his own window at dawn. Lottie might have kept herself from knowing what her sister surely didn't speak of, but the mate couldn't help knowing of it.

"Ah, that's where I differ." All this ah-ing was part of the mate's new manner, as practical master of his own romance. "Lottie's — like everyone else. And I shan't mind that, you see. It'll be a help." He waggled his forelock, where once he might have clapped Jim's shoulder. "But *she's* just right for *you,* you old dreamer. Whatever you do." This was the first casual reference to another decision — to split their business destiny — since the decision had been made. "So we're both satisfied."

It was the uneasiest conversation they had ever had between them, but still the mate lingered.

"Goes a bit heavy on the eats," he said. There was no doubt of course as to of which sister he spoke. He looked over at Jim — gawking there by the mantel-piece as if he was pinned to it. "But that's good for the milk then, Jim, isn't it?"

"The milk?" It took Jim a blush to understand. "I suppose," he said then, imitating the mate's heavy manner. "Seems to be I have heard that. Yes, I suppose. And beer too, they have to drink, don't they." Mercifully the phone rang — as it did a lot these days — interrupting this exchange on nursing mothers. From the way the mate answered, it was Lottie, and Jim signaled quickly, as usual, for the mate to take the car. A car was still conspicuous; he and Emily went shanks' mare. Lottie and the mate went much to restaurants. So, here too, as the mate said, everybody was satisfied.

Later though, to Emily, Jim spoke of his own doubts, though delicately, not mentioning the milk. For you must understand that though he and she might not be every conventionally plighted couple of those days, socially, just the same, they were living through a state of being which is almost unknown now. In those days, the "engagement period" was as much a part of the common experience, and with actions and emotions proper to it, as is today the

[195]

state of being divorced. It was the time when the male, being usually the less innocent, had to act it the more, while the woman formally took over the future of their days. Was he being less responsible than the mate? "Children — " he said. "Of course, we'll have them. But I have to tell you something." He hesitated. "I — never really think of them much. To tell the truth, I never think of them at all." Was he unnatural?

Truly there must have been few like her, for she only laughed, as he told the mate later. "It's because we daren't," she said. But a few more days later, speaking of her sister and the mate — which Jim didn't mention to the mate, though Lottie may have — she said, "I don't want to think about *them;* that's who I don't want to think of. I've told Lottie that!" Jim was left to wonder why, and to chalk it up to engagements. When he asked her, she said only again "I'd rather not think about them at all."

Despite which, the wedding was a double one. All the considerations which throng at such times had forced it. Counting in Oriskany, there were three houses to be disposed of, and two jobs. Here money came into it, with a bouncing surprise. The Pardees were indeed fairly poor now, but by the cleverly twisted will of a father not inclined to trust too long in horses or women, as soon as his daughters married men acceptable to the will's trusteeship — and who would doubt that Jim and the mate would be — each girl would be ten thousand dollars rich. It was a will which mightn't have held water if tried in court elsewhere — even as drawn by Sand Spring's most prominent lawyer, whose partner was a trustee — but recall that in those small days, the town was the court. After that disclosure, came the effects, each to each, of that much money. Oriskany, the mate's choice just as the idea of a garage had been, clearly fell to the mate; with Lottie's dowry he could buy it on his own — and begin. Jim liked the Pardee house well enough, the more so for its being on water; he and Emily would take it, with fair compensation to the other two of course, and think awhile whether to sell, or stay and somehow make use of the land. The mate, because of the needs of his house, would have to give up his surveyor's job; for the same reason, Jim would keep his factory one. The mate would need the car. All four would work together beforehand to put both houses in order, tidy for destiny — and dynasty. Jim's house, the house of the two men's bachelordom, would be sold.

When the news of all this came out, the two men found that they had in all ways disposed of themselves just as the town had estimated and favored they would — and that the town was now ready to make them part of the town. People of the type who always offer themselves to such processes soon did so, the lawyer's wife insisting on the use of her salon for the two weddings — both providentially without

[197]

family to crowd it — while a few miles away, the rector where Jim as a barge child had attended his longest spell of Sunday school, now held out his church. Both offers were accepted, for two-thirty in the afternoon and four-thirty respectively; if it was to be a round-robin affair, hadn't it been so from the beginning?

The night before the wedding, the mate took the car and went off by himself. Just before he left, he stood in the archway of the dining room, looking at Jim, who was at the table, picking over old correspondence he wasn't planning to take with him. The mate stared, until Jim looked up, inquiring. At this, the mate shook himself all over, as if out of sleep. "No," he said. "You wouldn't want to." Then he went out. Jim must have been asleep when the mate came in, and slept on so late the next morning that the mate, up bright and early nevertheless, had to wake him — or else perhaps the mate never went to bed at all.

On one of the rare, glorious afternoons then, which October in that region sometimes trails on into early November, the four participants assembled, attended by divers hats and feathers and waistcoats; among them, who should be there but the Skinners from Oriskany, the two veterans from Jim's factory and the mate's boss and apprentices, the banker, though without his wife who was too grand for it, and the librarian? — when one gets down to it, relations can always be found, on pre-winter Sunday afternoons, even eager to be. Their names and faces are darkness now, though the watch chains glow, the feathers still wave. Of the four principals, Emily was to be Lottie's bridesmaid, then Lottie, as the first bride, would serve as her matron of honor; each of the two grooms, serving as each other's best man, guarded in a pocket his friend's marriage-ring. There were no other attendants. Neither bride was to be formally dressed. The lawyer was to officiate at the first wedding in his own parlor; he was also a judge. Since it was a civil ceremony, no one gave the bride away, but the lawyer's wife came forward from the kitchen where she had been helping the maid with what was still called the "collation," on the way doffing her apron and putting on a hat and a pair of gloves. And now we are privileged to set aside the bare facts of forty years ago, and stare.

Lottie's dress, it can now be seen, was one step too pink, as if she had tried to go beyond the candy-pink which was always so becoming to her, and had stretched too far, toward blood. It was hot in the lawyer's high-ceilinged room with fireplace and furnace grate both running, and as the plump do, she sweated. The sweat was dainty enough, smelling of Sunday and fresh cotton knickers, but as the marriage service wore on between the four standing so close, the dark crescents under the bride's arms were the serum-pink of separated blood, and the smell of the new satin made a man think of rutting. She remained dainty yet, with her thoughts falling back into dells of sweetness, and the mate beside, shoulders bulging and neck throttled by his collar, was the dancing bear. But at the end, it was the bear, with that great cry of *Grandchildren!*, who spoke.

Then it was "clop-clop and away" to the rectory, or to whatever sound by a lawyer's Packard is made. If, on the way, anyone murmured, "Wouldn't if he'd said he could see his *children* be enough?" then there is an advantage to double weddings, in that a lot about them is strange. Meanwhile, what an artist memory is, at leaving out what is unimportantly important — the sound those wheels made — and bringing forward instead the sound of shanks' mare on gravel, as the rector leads us up the path and his wife doffs her apron and joins us! Emily, whose dress is unstained and as stiff as white icing, has chosen to be married in the church. The brief slice of afternoon between parlor and church is brilliant Finger Lakes weather, harvest weather, with the vines shorn but the grapes and pumpkins still gold and purple at every farmstall on the hills, and the cold November of Great Lakes weather still to come. It is the time when hills and water are in perfect balance here, that only time of the year. Inside the church, which has been warmed also, the four figures exchange places. The bride has a hat on, and this is only the chapel side of the church, but the Episcopal service falls in drapery behind her, folding back and back, like a wedding-train. A matron of honor in pink gives her away, or does what matrons do, very serviceably. This is a double-ring ceremony, but the mate and matron drop neither. Around these four, as the rector drones, the chapel gives its own responses. To the left, a high memorial window gave out the text And They Were Not Divided, in sun-dusty gothic citron and blue, but this meant death, and the four pairs of eyes turned casually away. Far back in the kind of history which got itself embossed in memorial windows, a pair were not divided even in death — but this had nothing to do with the couples here, at least now. Can you remember it, the time when death had nothing to do with you? — if *remember* can be called the proper word.

To the right of the two couples who were joined as if in a knot by the rector, there was another window as high and wide, but so shielded by a hanging of church velour dustily roped back near the floor, that what it shielded they never saw, maybe only the sun and the air, the light and the damp. Above the rector's head as it bent to them, but yards away behind it and lit with one votary lamp, the solid wall was incised with names whose worn gilding could not be read at that distance, though gold leaf was fresh on a text above. Throughout the ceremony, until the marriage-kiss, Jim's eyes kept returning to it. After the first congratulations were over, he went up to the wall, as he said "to see what war it was." The mate joined him there, and the rest of the party, already clustered at the church door, respectfully averted their attention from the two buddies, who were perhaps enjoying a last stray minute of bachelordom.

Together, the two men looked up at the text above the names. *Take what ye have,* it said, *and hold fast till I come.*

"Poor chaps," said the mate. " 'Take what ye have.' Well, *I'll* take it — now."

Jim nodded, staring at the text above. "I can wait," he answered it. "I'm not a soldier any more."

And it seemed to each of them that he spoke in his own voice.

The rector, coming up behind them, said, "It's the Civil War, the Civil. No part of this state had more Union dead than we did around here, did you know that? And hereabouts, this is the oldest church."

The two men nodded politely, and each took this moment to slip his ten dollars into the rector's hand.

As the party made ready to drive away from the church, few in it neglected to tell the young pairs that they had left their youth there. As the cars drew up again at the lawyer's door for the wedding-feast, some kinder soul, gazing up at the cold blue over the rooftop, where a short sunset was nipping westward, murmured, "Applejack weather, now."

"And I'll drink you under the table in it!" said the

mate, leaping out first, and almost bashing in the front door before it was opened to him.

Behind him, Lottie looked up at Jim and Emily as if, though married later than she, they were somehow her mentors still. "Will he really drink a lot of it?" she whispered. The mate heard her, and turned round. "I do a lot of everything," he said, leaving no echo to wonder what his bride did know of her Jim, except Emily's silently tucked smile, over what she knew of hers.

Do you know how applejack from that part of upstate New York — not from the wine-hills but from the apple orchards — is made, or used to be; how the full brew of all that's in it is frozen away from what won't freeze, leaving nothing at the core of the ice but the apple brandy, nothing but almost pure alcohol? At the wedding-feast, some of the younger people circulated a vintage bottle of it — last year's. In addition, two bottles of Great Western champagne were supplied by the lawyer's wife. In spite of this, the mate, when requested to sing, stood hard as a rock, though he would warble none of his home songs or any of those which made his voice sound tenor, and concluded with those ballads of the late war in which everyone, musician or not, could join him. "It's a long, long way to Tipper*aree*," they sang, "it's a long way, to go." And "How long, oolong," they sang, "you gonna be gone?" The songs all spoke in some such way, whether speaking of

[203]

absences or windups. "There's a long, long trail a-wi-yunding," the mate sang, "into the *land* of, my dreams," and the others answered him, "Where the *ni*-ightin-*gale* is *singing* and a *white*, moon, beams."

So then, they all drove away in the cars that everyone either owned or had borrowed, and for a while after, all the houses of guest and host and principals were lighted up, then dark again — from the Pardees' house on one side of Sand Spring, to the house in Oriskany, on the other. Only the little house waiting to be sold, the one where the two Jims had been, remained altogether dark. And it was a long, long time until morning.

For more than a week of nights and days, those honeymoon nights and days when it is allowable for no phone to ring or horn to toot in the driveway, it was a long time until morning, until the one when, at four o'clock of a cold hour, the door out at Pardees' house was pounded dead awake, and the two there, running down in their nightclothes, opened up to the sound of a car slipping away, and Lottie, fully clothed somehow or other, a shawl falling away from her, face dented and bloody, neck and arms bitten and scratched, as if she had met an animal in the woods, but the bloody marks dried brown, as if she had finally conquered it — fell through the door.

IV

S o, that's the windup, or the beginning of it, for
those four, who seem to me too young ever to become grandparents to a generation like yours. You,
standing here, only just old enough to be off to war
or marriage, seem to me far older than they, and I
shouldn't be surprised if you felt it; your youth
comes out in other ways. As for the forty years more
of the story, you know all of it except for these few
private parts of it now half exposed — plus whatever
two old men can finally tell you. All the rest of it, you
grew up with, and scarcely consider a story at all. It's
no news to you that the two Jims, though related to
some of you only through their wives, are called
"Grandfather" by all of you, so close are they to both
you and each other, though one still calls the other
"mate." Nor is it any skin off your noses that although Jim and Emily had a fine parade of four
children which surprisingly didn't begin until several
years after the marriage, and the mate had only one
solitary cub, conceived when we all knew — never-

theless, four out of the six grandchildren stem from the mate. This is the way, in daily life, matters even themselves.

That way, all the money the mate has made (not real tycoon wealth but the considerable estate, in company shares and accrued income, of a man who, during the Second World War, went from a small job in the Remington Arms Company to the directorship of small-arms contracts for its nearest rival) can be divided without strain, particularly since any farm he touches even in the most gentlemanly way, usually turns against him, into money too. Even then, big spender as he is on others, in the gifts that come up in him now and then like terrible belches, of generosity of course — like the sloop he gave Jim, who didn't any more want one than the barge it was supposed to take the place of, or the coat Emily could only wear once a year on the New York City vacation, for who can wear mink in Sand Spring? — even then their brother-in-law, as he is still known to the town, is hard put to it to spend his money, maybe because his own home expenses are so small. For I suppose it never occurs to you — or has one of the women in the family told you, no doubt very romantically? — why your richer grandfather lives on in the small house that his friend brought him home from the wars to, in the twenties, the house which was once scheduled to be sold?

Meanwhile, if Jim and Emily's two grandchildren,

with their parents, aunts and uncles before them, can only look forward to the glass-shelved mahogany bookcases and modestly solid silver of a first-class Sand Spring Dutch Colonial built circa 1935, then it doesn't matter anyway, since the second generation are all associated in a family business which no one would presume now to call matriarchal, and this generation in turn has only two to whom to hand it down. For anyone in town who assumes, as many do, that the mate has money in the Aswami Baking Company — put there at some time or other, either when it began, or in one of the crises which small businesses have, or when it was finally incorporated — is wrong. Emily and Jim could never have let him put a cent in it. After that night they couldn't be in debt to him, and there must be no more partnership. In this way, Jim expresses silently his lifelong pity for his friend, to whom he expresses aloud only his equally and lifelong sincere admiration. And Emily, in her woman's way or merely in Emily's, was left free to expiate to herself or approve — whoever knew which with Emily? — what she would *not* do, that night or ever, for her sister, and indeed considered herself to have done for the mate. In this way, the three could remain as close as you have always known them to be. For no matter what tales you may have heard or not bothered to hear, only now is it becoming clearer, now that two old men have talked, how the four of them became three.

Forty years ago or four hundred, to take in a
woman bloody and beat from her husband, must be
the same. They would bind her and bathe her, and
once it was plain that no doctor was needed, perhaps
when she had been fed and was asleep, then those
two, still in their nightclothes and maybe with the
tender muckiness of their own love still upon them,
would sit down. The facts which later became common knowledge to the four of them (and only them)
were these. Lottie's wounds had only been surface
ones; what with the dents and puffs and a few streaks
of blood that could well be spared, it was only what
another pair might have done in a night's fierce
cleaving — but made strange by the shawl and the
hour, and that she had come at all. To say nothing of
who had brought her. The mate had brought her,
though under whose duress she did not say. For
though restless at first — yes, that is the word —
once she was tidy and had her tea in front of her, she
appeared so calm and settled, so much in her right
mind or like her usual self, that though this was odd
for the circumstances, they scarcely knew what to
ask. He "came after" her, she told them, then she
smiled at them as if they should surely understand
this, kissed them each on a cheek and went, with her
light, bouncing tread that never showed her weight,
into her old room. But what did she expect them to
do?

When they phoned the mate, at first there was no

answer, though they had given him time to reach home. He couldn't answer at first, he told them later; he couldn't bear to, because of the way they knew him, and he them. If he'd been a stranger, he said, he could have had it out with them — their bewilderment, or Jim's — and his rage. He himself, he said, was never bewildered. "From the first hour," he said, "I knew what I was up against." Then he too said no more. But that was later, when they saw him. Over the phone, when at last they reached him, he said only, "No, I won't come after her," but it must have been chance that he used those words, surely meaning only that he chose not to come and get her, at least not just now.

"Are you — all right yourself, mate?" said Jim. What a thing to have to ask!

"No sight for the marketplace," said the mate; then he couldn't go on; he made the queerest sound that said he couldn't, and hung up.

While Lottie went on sleeping, the other two conferred.

"It can't be — could it be —" said Jim, "that she just didn't *know* about it — ?" He said afterward that here, even as late as this, an edge of humor hovered — what a riot if it was merely that, then just give the pair time and all would be well, or as with the half the world not as lucky as some, at least smoothed over.

"No, of course not!" said Emily. "We kept horses."

"Well, what the devil — then — ?" he said, slow to anger as always. And why he should have been angry at *Emily*, he wondered after. "He's a man, that's all. I know the mate. A bit quick, maybe. And maybe one for the wom — never mind. But he's no brute. I'd swear it." He looked at her square. "And I can."

If she flinched at that, he said he couldn't tell it. She spoke softly, "I can't say what men are, the way you can, or what women are. But I daresay you're right." It was a long speech, for Emily. "And I know Lottie," she said.

"Then — if you knew what — why didn't you —? Why didn't you say something?" How absurd! — he could see that himself — and that they two should be quarreling about it. He never would again, he said after. For she stopped him cold, even if she didn't mean to.

"I'm only a girl," she said.

And she was too — not twenty yet. People like Emily — he said to the mate later — when they do speak, how they go to the heart of it!

"And why wouldn't she," the mate answered, "for that's how *you* are, Jim."

Anyway, when they saw him, that was maybe the worst shock of all. Lottie was gone by that time, taken by Jim down to Troy, to that woman friend she stayed with until Lottie found herself pregnant, some old maid friend. It couldn't be said that Lottie had been deeply wounded that her sister wouldn't keep her on and allow her to take up her old life there; she had been a little hurt of course, but mostly — surprised. But they didn't speak of her for a moment, now that they saw him.

"The eye I did myself," he said. "On the bedpost." Then there was the blue dent on his temple, which you all know, which never did go away. The scratches were nothing, he said. But one or two had festered; the human nail will do that. Emily went at once to get a basin, though it was two weeks since that night, and more.

"Thank you, Jim," said the mate, while she was out of the room. "And let's not speak of it again, of what or why, unless we have to." He managed a smile. "Maybe someday, when we're old." He put the familiar hand on Jim's shoulder. "There's just something I want to ask Emily."

When she returned, he asked her it, in the middle of her sponging his face. She had put a towel round his neck and was treating his cuts as firmly as any trainer. The iodine made him squint his good eye. His voice wasn't much, not for him.

"When was it, Emily?" he said. "That you decided."

"Decided what?" she said, but they all knew, just as the mate must have known at once that it would have been Emily's force which had refused her sister; Jim on his own could never have done it.

"When I saw her walk into her room," said Emily

slowly. "When I saw her walk like that, back into her old room."

The mate nodded, holding his face up to the washcloth, his eyes closed against the water; then he opened them so that she might look into them; he and she were a pair, both of them quick to seize people and size them, not long bewildered. Then he jumped up and went to the mirror.

"About my sister," she said to his back. "There's nothing to Lottie . . . except — what one sees."

"And if she were my sister," he said without turning, "I'd have seen it."

His voice was bitter. For we're so trained up to believe, Christian and infidel both, that *all* people are like icebergs, the greater part of them *beneath*. Why must we forget or deny that there are these others, too?

"Why . . . Emily — " said Jim. "Why — Jim." He rarely called the mate by their common name. "She's right, do you see? And — if we could — remember it. Wouldn't — could that make it easier?"

The mate turned from the mirror, slowly, fingertips still to the stickingplaster he'd been dabbed with. "For *whom?*"

Emily only looked at them both with her level glance. The mate came up to her, his head cocked the way one has to with an eye puffed closed. "Maybe I'm like that too," he said. "Nothing to me, except what you see."

"Not if you can say it," said Emily, and Jim with a nod agreed.

All three were silent for some minutes. Then the two men both shook their heads, like dogs out of water, away from this kind of talk. "Well — I'm off," said the mate. Instead, he rested the palms of his hands stiff-armed on the table and stared down into its center. "Got to admit it though, I'm dashed. I'm a bit — dashed."

Maybe that's why he's had to be the opposite, ever since.

"I'm making her an allowance, of course," he said. "But I don't plan to go down there after her."

"But otherwise — " said Jim.

"Otherwise . . . I'll have to sell Oriskany. It's her money bought it." He looked at them as squarely as his eye allowed him. "Maybe I'll sell it to you."

He did always have a business head, even at odd times. Of course they both smiled at the idea, Emily the more.

"But if she'll come back — " said Jim, poor Jim, always seeking to make his kind of peace, or to find out what that was.

"Something may come of it." The mate spoke lightly. Then he screwed his face the way a person does when he intends to look mean. "Something . . . may . . . come of it all. We'll wait and see."

Something did of course, the child. And though in these days, a woman mightn't have come back to have it, Lottie did — maybe a Lottie always would. Later he said that he would have divorced her otherwise, but that's blarney; the mate would never divorce the mother of his child, and that's how it's worked out, hasn't it? — in the mate's own way. For, during the months before the child came, it was a sight to see, how he cossetted her, bringing her up breakfast before he went off to the job he'd decided to hold on to, going against the doctor, to push her to eat. And to look at Lottie, though she didn't appear to give much thought to the baby itself that was coming, or even to her having it, everything was smooth as cream. It was repellent, maybe, to see a man use what he knew of his wife to get what he wanted out of her — which was dynasty — and maybe the mate himself knew it was, beneath that blind, horn-forward stare which always came on him when he was after something. And he got him, by God — the lone boy who was dynasty and is dead now, but not before he in turn fathered four of his own; can it be fifteen years now, and the war *after* the second world one in its turn an old one? And the mate has him still — however way many of us are conceived; here we are — or were. And here you are, the fruit of us, burdened with the tale.

Once the baby was born and coddled out of its two-month frailty, everyone knew that things were going badly out at Oriskany. It dragged on so for a few months more, then ended, though there was no more violence, at least as far as was let be seen. Then Lottie left again, this time very quietly, by what private arrangements were never publicly known. That she had made some agreement was taken for granted since, though she made no more forays on her sister, indeed not even a letter so far as was known, she wasn't the sort to manage alone. Then indeed the town could reflect back on how the mate had always been the doting parent and the mother the negligent or perhaps confounded one — and could take the mate to its bosom. For Lottie had left behind the child.

So — the mate never got his garage, or Jim either — though that too remains to be explained. Oriskany was sold — it's funny now to think of the mate having to sell a place to get money — and the money presumably reverted, from a distance, to "the mother," as the town has since persistently referred to her, always in hushed tone. The mate moved nearer Jim, so that Emily could tend his child, which was subsequently brought up during the day with her others, joining its father at night. And that's why such a rich grandfather lives in such a small house; half of reality has these kindergarten reasons for it — this being part of the general undertow and sneakwork of the world. Surely it's also why, when we can see a trolley ride clear, we cling to it.

If Lottie got the best or the worst of things, the town never precisely knew, nor could they tell whether Jim and Emily knew either. At first she was heard of quite simply and normally, as working in a bakery down in Troy. The bakery was in character, and not only in hers — you watch. Later they heard she was working in a similar capacity in the town of North Adams, Massachusetts — and the migration of people, by foot or wheel or hunger, is always interesting — for there is no other town in the state of Massachusetts which more resembles a New York State town called Troy. Why a woman whom surely the mate supported, and who had had ten thousand dollars of her own in the bargain, should need to work in such places, only those who saw her could say. Bulletins got vaguer as times got leaner, and if it was heard that she had invested her money in oil stock and lost it, others had done the same. There was shock when some vacationer reported seeing her in a place called Squaw Village, not what it might sound but one of those tourist places on the Molly Stark trail, with a big country store and Indian tepee setups; the shock was that she had let her hair grow down in a braid, dyed black surely, to add to her squaw-weight, and was on charade in the gifts-and-goodies shop, billed as the mother of an Indian family, in a troup of hired braves and papooses selling everything from carnival glass to saltwater taffy. "Surrounded by *children!*" the shocked vacationer said. By which it could be seen that our town, like many in the region, had in some ways maintained its own character.

Then, in the forties somewhere, it heard for sure — or at least from her — that she was rich again or very comfortable; the oil stock — think of it, oil stock bought by a Lottie! — had panned out after all. It was in Florida that some folks met her; by this time we upstate farmers, and business people too, were wintering in Florida ourselves, and not bus-ing it down there either, flying there, just like the birds. She was very dressy now — the women of the party said — in a way that hid her bulk, and like a well-heeled widow with her bracelets and gold charms. She lived in one of the warm coastal towns where the older boat-crowd sat a lot on deck or by the water, her distinction being, and maybe her respectability too, that she didn't drink — diabetes had lost her a toe. "Didn't *drink*," the women said. "Dressed like Rochester, sure, but there's that bazoom to make you think of Miami," some of the men said. Others said, "Oil stock, nuts, anybody knows what he's worth now, and he's never divorced her, that's all." The wildest tale of all, which should encourage us all as to the civic imagination, was that the mate himself had been seen down there, in that hotel like a French château, coming out of a suite behind her or her image, in the wee hours of the morn. A lovely conclusion, only not possible. True enough, that he's often seen down there at that place or others, and that he goes to some trouble to see that the middle-aged tarts he chooses will look to strangers as if they could be his wives. Seeing him at a table, bending his fine head of white hair very courtly over some nice, fullblown woman with not much makeup and good manners, who'd think otherwise — unless the real wife was known to the observer from before? It may be that he was showing the lady out of his suite all right, and treating her like one — whoever she was. But it wasn't Lottie. To dream of Lottie as her husband's whore or anyone else's is to — well no, it's neither to laugh nor to cry. It's to wonder how a woman who hadn't it much in her to stir the emotions, could hold a man down, and for a lifetime too, and by emotions he never had it in him to have. If to be that is to be a whore, then, poor thing, she was one. But there are those who say she never could have been one conventionally, not even with him. How do they know? Because, though it's said she used to see the boy now and then — for his own good, as maybe Emily insisted — she never came back to Sand Spring, not once. If she'd been a whore somewhere, rich or not, she could have come back to town — and been respectable.

Now Emily, though for her there is no key. For, all her life, unlike the other three, each of whom wanted something in a way which overpowered or colored

them — Emily was concerned with the workings of
daily living only, and so her mystery, like its, is only
hinted at here and there in the shadows and gildings
of that ordinary living, and is as hard to see. When
the mate, one solemn day, carried his baby into her
house to be cared for forever, although she had none
of her own even begun yet, she received the infant
handily, yet not greedily, in no doubt that her own
babies would come along, when called. Though it
was a sad day, to the two men watching she left no
doubt either that in any day where such a child was,
there were still tweaks of joy. The three things she
said might have come one by one out of a casket of
the sort women keep by them. To the mate, whose
face, except for the blue dent, was now healed to an
even hardness, she said lightly, "Don't fret, don't
fret" — whereas to the baby cradled in her arms she
said almost formally, "It can't be helped." Shouldn't
it have been the other way round? Or did she hope
to make the little man see as early as possible a view
of the world — her sex's — in which, if he grew up
like the rest of his, he would never believe? Or was it
simply that she was one of those who from birth
know the position of the generations and can act by
it, needing no other compass or calendar.

But in the third thing (which was Lottie's epitaph
no matter how much might be said of her later)
surely there was also a hesitance in the way Emily

spoke, as if some of the verdict — in the way character is apportioned among families, or among women
— must surely cling to herself.

The three were sitting in the bay window, out at
Pardees'. Coffee was on the table, tea for the mate. In
the nearer depths of the house, the baby had been
put down; its next bottle was ready on the stove. The
stove was Bismarck. On the lake in front of the house
it was late August again, one of its lizard-gray days,
scaly with mist, from which autumn bursts like a
pumpkin, a fruit. All three couldn't help but be
thinking how far, from Bismarck to baby, they had
come. Outside, on the railless water, the fogline now
and then parted a few feet above it in porcelain
flushes of vision to which each pair of eyes would
put a personal shape. Over her own, Emily's brows
almost met, but it was she who first broke the long
pause, though silently, flinging her baby-tired arms
wide. She could do that — it was one of the things that
made her seem tall, yet contrarily could bring her
fingertips in again to hold an eyelash; she had
stretched her legs wide and closed them again, and
in the nutcracker between them brought herself a
man. She looked at him now, at Jim watching the
water, loving his vagueness, never scolding, perhaps
tending it — for both their ends. But today was the
mate's day; anything about Lottie belonged to him.

"Jim — " she said. The two men always knew
which Jim she meant. She spread her hands — like a

sister's — then clasped them. "The sugar-people. That's the way they are."

Each nodded at her, needing no further explanation. Jim, her husband, smiled. It wasn't his day, life hadn't marked him outwardly yet, as it had the mate, but until his inner arguments settled themselves, until he could point to the mark on himself perhaps, his clever girl would always have a word for what the risks were, and the responsibilities. He, meanwhile, was waiting. And there was no shame in it.

It could have been only a few minutes later when she got up, walked over to the great stove, cold as armor these many months in favor of the smaller summer one, and put her hand on it. "I've been thinking," she said. Her clear eyes shone with a forward-backward light. "There's not a decent baking company in town."

The genius of it was that from the first she had said "company." A mere bakery, even if its owners keep in the basement a staff of two floured German madmen — do you know bakers? — is still only a shop. Nevertheless, that's the way they began of course, but with that other word always leavening the conversation and at last rising from it, written neater than Nebuchadnezzar's — on the wall. The name "Aswami" came from a secondhand truck which glimmered at them from a car-lot when they were on holiday up near the Canadian border — "The Aswami Baking Company" — the name of its past owner and locale conveniently obliterated, but an Indian version after all. In the early years, toward her thirties, Emily, selling at the shop's counter — did she ever think of her sister? — or downstairs, scarf-headed, checking over the staff in the large basement of the second establishment, or at Jim's side at an evening party, looked ever younger, almost a child-wife — you'll remember there was almost a decade between them. As for the parties, the two of them, if by choice not in the forefront, were always on the list now, having long since moved to the middle of town and got over their trouble.

In later years, in the business office of the factory they built on a razed property — yes, in Oriskany — as Jim grew more portly, Emily, though no plumper herself, kept matronly pace with him somehow. The children, when they came, were never vulgarly underfoot in the shop, a distaste for this being part of what her livery-stable heritage had taught her, so that by the time the company had been achieved, the children, now parents themselves, could laughingly tell their own, home from prep and boarding schools with perhaps a schoolmate, that *they* had never even had as many cakes and cookies as children normally did, when young. All of *them* called their parents Jim and Emily, oddly modern for them, unless one suspected that in this way the mate's child wouldn't have been shunted away from "Mother" to "Aunt Emily." For which reason — far back in those browndark days of childhood which precede the light-blazed ones on which young men's planes go down (their last letters to dear Emily arriving later) — it had been done. As for the baking products on which this small, decent empire has been built, these have kept pace with modernity too; the company has one of the best bread to doughnut lines in the up-state area, all properly packed with no more than 10 per cent preservatives — and there isn't a fritter in the lot. But what with automobiles and trucking, and the trackless wastes between towns and appetites, always needing to be covered, it has done very well.

Dear Emily — as much more than old letters still say. If we don't count that young man, the father of some of you (and how does one count death out of one's generation, when it is not among the natural and daily?), then Emily was the first of us to die. She is the first to fall, of that young constellation, and never will there be a better reason for you all to gather here. As might be expected of such a woman, she went from one of the commoner diseases, which was gotten to, as the doctors like to say, in time. When Jim took the mate with him to help order the stone, and they stood in the stonecutter's office, studying that grim manual of texts and design cuts, looking out the window at his samples, it was the mate who suddenly slammed the book closed and said "What do I do in my *business*, when I buy anything! Let's go to an *expert!*" So they hopped in that other car of his, the Bentley he'd got from England — the two men when they go out together always use his cars — and drove to the church.

Time being what it is, the rector was now a young seminarian. And no worse for it, said the mate, to whom it was smart business for the old to deal with the young — who as he said would have everything at their fingertips. Since it was Jim's wife who had died, the young minister deferred to him, and couldn't have been kinder or taken longer to help search out what Jim thought suitable for a wife like that, and a stone. Neither of the two old men walked over to look at old Civil War names, wars being too new again, but if Jim's search took the long, trembling time it did, this was because he remembered what he had once said in this place.

" 'I can wait,' " he said to the mate. "Do you remember?" And it seemed to him that now, now if ever must be the time to express all that he had been gathering for a lifetime and had never expressed properly, about our place in the world here and his modest place also; now if ever was the time to say it all. But though dozens of texts were brought forth, there was none that satisfied him. It came time for evensong, but the mate didn't press him. The young man, though nobody had come for the service, was going round quietly, turning on lights and so forth, being his own sexton. And suddenly he was stopped in his sweeping. "What's behind that curtain?" the mate said. "I wondered, at the time."

That young man almost fell over his broom, he was so eager; he had seen the Bentley. It must have been hard on him to accept a church so hopelessly faded in congregation as that one, and as you may have noted at today's dedication, though he very kindly returned for it, he has since been called elsewhere. But he had everything at his fingertips that day. "There were to have been two," he said, pointing to the high memorial window opposite the curtained one. "But something happened." Then he pulled back the curtain. The day was one of the short, winter ones, no anniversary of an autumn one and no sunset, but between the darkness outside and the light within, the blank pane perhaps showed up best. So that is how come, two years later almost to the day, which the stained-glass people told us was optimum — Emily's window. The mate wanted to pay for it, but of course that couldn't be, even though he was the one to persuade Jim to have it.

"She wouldn't have wanted such a thing," said Jim.

"In some ways, Jim," said the other old man, "I — other people — knew her better than you did!"

Then the young man put his hand between them. It was the nearest they had ever come to an out-and-out difference of opinion, not to say quarrel.

"She was a *common* woman, a *homely one*," said

Jim. "Words change, but when I was a boy, that's what the mourners used to say at barge funerals, of any woman who had the human touch to her, and had brought with her all the home comforts, during a lifetime that wasn't never nothing but daily." He looked ashamed then, either at his grammar or his eloquence, but with him who can tell? "She was an ordinary woman," he said. "She was a nonpareil."

"I know what you mean, Jim," said the mate. "Even without going to one of your dictionaries. I know what you mean." How he could remember! "You mean — she was like everyone else."

So, between them, that was her epitaph — though when it came to the window, they finally left it to the rector, after all. He chose "Many Waters"; I suppose you know it. Of course you do, with the window, how could you not? "Many waters cannot quench love, neither can the floods" — and so forth. Maybe the mate did help suggest it because of all the water in it, knowing Jim's tastes or thinking he still did — remember that sloop! And it is a beautiful verse.

"So it is, mate," said Jim. "So it is, Jim." Calling the mate by name was meant to repair the sharp words. "But you know something?" He stared through the blank pane at the dark land outside it. "This is a mixed region, around here. I see it more and more."

Later, when he saw first the window itself, back at the glassmakers' of course, not at the unveiling, he both nodded his head and shook it, even though the figure rising from the water in all its blood-reds and milky whites was an angel, not Emily. "Funny thing," he said. "I always see her . . . *from* the water. *On* the land."

And now Jim. He was fond of saying that if there was something he wanted to know about himself he could always go to the mate for it. The mate, if he was there to hear him, always remarked, "Same here. Only, *he* won't tell." For forty years or more their lives had been twined together, but in such a way that if one showed himself ready to drown, the other didn't go down with him but held him; they weren't twins, unless twins can be of totally different temperament. The mate had his Floridas, and did or didn't speak of them. In the early years, the three sometimes had had to speak among them of Lottie, though never of the mate's long undivorcement itself; during the years when Emily did get a letter or two, these were spoken of, but curiously, only in twosome, either of the men to Emily or to each other, but never in threesome; after Emily's death, the other sister was not spoken of at all. In money matters, the town had at various periods thought it remarkable that the pair never minded who was the richer, but the friends themselves knew that too much teetering had gone on in that direction, ever for them to feel constraint. During the stunned years when the mate clung to his job like a man who has forgotten what his hands are holding, then it was

Jim, the ever solider townsman, who lent him money for unspecified needs, and it was only during the Second War — at a time when the limits of a small business, if these don't soar, are likely to be fixed — that the mate began to stumble forward, to climb as if he knew there was a top, and finally to claw to it. Until then, Jim, with his strong figure, hair faded and thinned but not balded, and his busy little cockerel of a wife beside him, had looked the younger of the two; now it was the mate, with the powder-white hair which had once been raven, and the kind of tycoon charm which can demonstrate in a handshake that it has known what it is to be shy. Jim, by now, had a particular kind of townsman's face, relaxed but puzzled in repose, the quality which in a younger man is called willing-to-learn. But — as you may have noticed — we haven't yet got solely and wholly to Jim.

For the curious thing about Jim was that one always got to him best through others, which may be why he persisted in claiming that he never quite knew himself. He wasn't an enigma, any more than any of us, but he had thought it his duty to face the world's enigma and study it — or he had always meant to; this meant that if he could wait, others must watch. Why was it otherwise that though he and Emily stood all their lives in handfast, Jim, as against the mate, seemed the more divided? He never minded being in business with a wife, even such a competent one, and never consented to lose dignity for it — though a town will try. The town could do nothing with him or to him, while he studied it. He had his hobbies then, not too cranky ones for a self-styled reflective; about the time he married, for instance, he seemed to give up books at large — or the timid taste which had been tending that way — only to replace them with a collection of dictionaries which, all along unknown to himself, may have been what he had been going to the libraries for. For a while it would seem as if he never read these either, for it was at this period that he took to collecting the names of towns on matchboxes, merely for the way they pleased or teased the something within him which he couldn't explain otherwise; when he drove the highways on a trip to Yellowstone for instance, passing through a state he would chant some such refrain to the children: South Bend, Plymouth, Mishawaka, Peru. But that was only when the children were small, and he could think he was teaching them America. After one particular Christmas, he and the mate tried to tinker over a hobby together; do you ever remember your parents telling you of a year when both Jim and the mate came back from separate trips to New York City — with toy trains? But it didn't last long, and here they did share a likeness; if, like most, as they

[229]

got older, they wanted only the more to see the world and to grasp it, then this wasn't their style of miniature.

Curiously enough, as their teeter-totter went now up, now down, it was the mate who had begun to educate himself with books — real books. He would do it on his own terms of course, when and if he felt he could get to them, and in his own character — which he so well knew. In just the same way, before a certain trip abroad, he had gone to a language school and demanded they teach him French in ten minutes — which they did, if poorly, and to a dancing school where, in somewhere double the time, he did well. Why he had been moved to do this for a trip with Jim on which they never got to do either of those things, did stay a mystery to him, until Jim told him.

"Why do you suppose I ever suggested that trip?" the mate asked, long after it was over.

"For old time memory's sake," Jim replied.

By that time, like most people, they were pretty good at memory, and each was able to swallow Jim's lie — for what they had gone for was to help shake from them the real death of youth, of the mate's son — not to remember their own. And from that trip Jim did bring back a huge terrestrial globe, lighted from within and girdled with half-life size figures clasping it, the gods of antiquity, holding it up with their spread arms and thighs. He found it in a stationer's in the Strand and had it sent home in sections for his collection: sometime back, he had gone on from his towns, and from America too, to globes. But when brought home, though it glowed as magnificently in the home as in the shop, instead of adding to his collection it ended it, for here the thing was, great with history and glass jewels too — did I say it was sixteenth-century and Venetian? — and even in Sand Spring it was only a globe. That ended all his collections except — as he said to the mate, spinning the globe for him, interpreting its yellowed mapskin by its own inner light, at dusk of a cold Sunday — except for one. From now on, he said, he would collect only the intangible, where a man had more chance.

"Will you look at that expression of his!" said Emily, watching him. "Worse than the children!" How she always watched, and the mate too — and how they knew him! For himself, he could decide best who and what he was, he always said, in the way *she* spoke to him. For, though often she said to him exactly what she had said to the mate and the mate's baby, on the day when they all had first to face up to things — over the years she had reversed these in tone. When she said, "Don't fret, don't fret now," it was as if to a wise child who knows that beforehand, but when she said, "It can't be helped, can it," she spoke as if to a strong man who bore with the world. As for the children, Jim always said they

[231]

loved him too much, that likely if he had done more in the world, they wouldn't have. He often said it. So here, maybe if only to help complete the circle within which a family is always judging itself, he was for once heard to participate in his own measurement.

And here we all are now: the four of us — two old men accountably present, and two women accountably absent — plus a listener or two now dogging their footsteps, from the crowd of them once upon a time at their knees. Between a last ride and a first memorial, the distance never changes, though opinions vary on the length of it, some memories going by wheel, others by wing. But all of us are here now, and ready to go back.

V

THE day the two old men went back was a day un-colored by water or breeze, tempered only with its meaning to them. As one gets older, this happens to days generally, but on that particular one the friends were driving back upstate from the glassmakers' studio in New Jersey, where they had gone for that private viewing, and now, no matter the weather they passed, the window's high, fragile rainbow overhung the highway in front of them. There is one stretch of the New York State Thruway that nine times out of ten is leaden with Catskill storm-weather, and this they did finally comment on — that neither had ever seen it in sunshine. Then the miles and the signposts took over again, and the silence — and always up ahead of them over the car's hood, above the spot where small figureheads were once attached at the radiator caps, that high transparency at the prow.

"Glass," said Jim. "I'll never understand how it's made. From *sand*."

The mate didn't answer at once. He was driving the Cadillac, in which he always kept the air-conditioner going, and the air they breathed was as pure and excellent as an engine accessory could make it, but voices were hollow. On Jim's side, a sign said NEXT EXIT and gave the number of miles.

"Want to stop?" asked the mate. They had been driving for some time.

"No, not unless you do," Jim answered, and the mate nodded. One of the latter-day satisfactions of their friendship, and no longer the lightest, was that physically they had kept pace with each other, neither's digestion or bladder being weaker than the other's.

"This exit we're coming to," said the mate. "We go off it, we could go on over to Skaneateles, have one of those big dinners at Krebs, and still get home."

"Krebs," said Jim. "Haven't heard that name in maybe — must be twenty-five years."

"Neither have I, come to think of it; maybe it isn't there." They drove on, and in a short time, too short if they met a cop, went by that exit.

"On the other hand," said the mate. "On the other hand, I've had to do a lot of driving around in our part of the state recently. Looking for a factory site. Cheap unoccupied land is getting harder and harder to find." He laughed. "I told the company directors — 'I got a couple of farms you can have, at a price.

I'll never live on 'em.'" By now the corporation drawl he adopted for business had become almost natural to him, and he could say a thing like that about farms without blinking. But he could surprise himself still, and Jim too. "Anyway, struck something when I was going around — came upon something I want to show you. You game?"

"Sure, why not. Just say how far, if I should phone. That housekeeper will wait dinner otherwise."

The mate moved his head to look at him, turning on him the bachelor stare of a man who ate in restaurants, and had argued housekeepers and other points too, with Jim.

"Guy behind you wants to pass," said Jim, but it wasn't the mate's driving that bothered him; the mate always had one eye on the road.

"Let her cook it," said the mate, "we'll get there. Though how you can want to tie yourself down like that — " He increased the speed which momentarily he had let slacken. "No, it's not far. Given a decent road — " He gave a short laugh. "Well, if it had one, I wouldn't have gone there and found it. Even so, in this thing, can't be more than an hour from home. Just that you have to go round it."

Where, to two natives of the district, could anything unknown to them be so close? But Jim didn't ask it, as the signposts traveled by. The mate drove on silently, until the definitive one, where they left the highway. Then he spoke, when it was no longer needed.

"It's on the way to Batavia," he said.

When they got there, they sat in the still car for a moment, then with one accord each opened the door on his side, stepped out, and turning on his heel, regarded it — sky, tumbled-in roofs, mossy underbrush to treetop glory — all. The windshield of the Cadillac was extra-wide, but there was too much ruin and growth here ever to be encompassed by it. Was cheap land for progress always so beautiful? They numbered it with their eyes — here outbuildings whose flat tops had melted into moss, there a great curved hangar of swallows' nests, on whose leaning timbers only fantasy tipped a weathercock, pointing not crazily, into the wood. All the facilities were here. And here was the hill, all the inhabitants of that village-for-a-day — except these two — long since piped back into it. It stood there like the massive bulk of their lives. Only those others were gone — and the steel rails.

The Little Otselica was running. One of the men — it didn't matter which — leaned down to it as if to stroke it for choosing to, then when his knee cracked, stood up shamefaced.

"Must have had a wetter season than we thought," said the other, but it didn't matter who, or if both saw the impress of a bather, her piled hair floating the water. The time had now come for memory to be the same.

Each of them found a stony stump to sit on, or a porous stone.

"Going to put your factory here?" said the one.

The other shook his head. With a wrist flick he waved aside the hill, annihilated it. "No problem there. But still the same trouble. Place still doesn't *go* anywhere."

But this was only the preamble. In the uneasy stillness, the nose of the Cadillac, parked in grasses, reared alert. And after a while, one of the men began at the beginning.

" 'Rushing the growler,' " he said. "Know what a 'growler' was? Came across it only the other day."

"No. Never even heard the word, except from you."

"Must have used them when they wanted to get there in a hurry. Eighteen-sixty-five, the dictionary said. Funny how it leaped right out at me. It's a horse-drawn cab."

The other tinkled his car keys against the stone. "It's all transport," he said, and drew a flask of brandy out of a hip pocket.

They had a tipple.

"Applejack weather," said the one holding the flask, staring behind the trees, where should be a sunset. Though there wasn't, the other nodded agreement; he too could smell the air of youth here, that pure autumn alcohol.

They had another.

The one got up from his seat, rubbed his backside and took off his coat to spread it on the ground.

"Damp," said his companion.

"Got me a sweater on." This was plain enough, but he looked at the coat on the ground a long while, before he finally sat on it, hugging his knees. "Tell me something," he said then. "Surely now it's all right for me to ask — and you to tell it." He looked down at ground between his legs. "It was her, wasn't it, you really wanted, Emily." He looked up at the other, asking it maybe only for her memorial.

But the other couldn't give it. "No," he said. Whether this was true or not, nobody would ever get anything else out of him. "I knew from the first . . . that it — " He finished the swallow left in the flask, and tossed it on the ground. "But it was Lottie I heard."

Then he shifted on his stone and looked down at his companion. "Anyway, I always thought — You and she. When you went off into the woods like that."

The other glanced up at his friend, then away. Did his friend really want to listen, to what he almost yearned to tell him? "I don't mind telling you it," he said at last, scoring the grass at the coat's edge with a forefinger. "Don't we almost have to tell it, now?"

He told it, putting in as well all he could of what
had passed through his mind then, or had been
huddled over through the years later — all he
wanted to understand and had waited for. Was this
its moment?

When he had finished, the other wasn't staring at
the trees any more, but at him. "'I can wait,' you
said," he said. "I always wondered why you said it.
When you already had it."

And maybe that was part of her memorial. But the
man on the ground, on the coat, sat wondering how
friendship, even with the help of wars and time and
family, could ever have knitted him to this other so
different one.

And the man on the stone swung the car-keys in
the arc of a surveyor's instrument, thinking the same.

"And the time *she* came," the one on the coat
finally said. "To our door. We always wondered, of
course. What really happened between you." He
paused. "You don't have to tell it. Not even now."

The man on the stone got up then and walked
away, stretching his arms, presenting his back. "No, I
want to. Somebody should know. And maybe, even if
I got marked early by it — maybe that was something."

"Sure is," said the man on the ground, staring at
his own greed to know, to be marked out — against
which even happiness, or even its memorial, were
not quite enough.

[239]

The other came back to his stone and sat on it again. He leaned forward confidentially, as over a business deal, but it was a time before he spoke. "It wasn't so much that she wouldn't do it. Couldn't. For love — or for sex either. Though I made her. Or even that she had to . . . to eat . . . even *during*. I caught her with a candy in her mouth — the first time." He paused, easing his collar, "I think I even knew how it would be, before I ever touched her. The night before the wedding, I knew. Even though, up to the wedding, I'd never done any more than put my tongue in her mouth. She liked that. But there was never any — we always went to restaurants. But I knew, that night. The minute you touch another woman, you know. But the night before — what can you do?" He fell silent.

The other nodded quietly, until something else occurred to him. "But — it *wasn't* that?"

His friend leaned his white forelock on his hand. "It can make you want it that way, that kind of — a man can form a taste for it. Or some could say he had it all along. A man doesn't always know his own tastes in that direction. Though I thought I did." He rubbed his face between his palms, and thus cleansed, clasped them again. "It was because I found out — how she *would* do it." He cleared his throat. "For a treat," he said. "For food."

The words echoed, though there were other

sounds all around and over them, the soft, meaning-
ful sounds of man-deserted country, that cracking of
twigs with which the woods take over, the callings of
birds.

"That day she came to you," he continued. "That
day, I'd locked her in. Starved her. She could afford
to. At nighttime, I unlocked her. And that — was
that."

"She told us that she started to walk over by
herself," said the other, "and that after a while she
heard a car behind her, and it was you. Never another word why. That's all she said, ever."

The other man stood up again, hands gripped in
his pockets. His rich voice, a singer's voice, was
small. "I unlocked her. And she *came* to me. She
offered it." A red went up his throat, to his cheeks, to
the blue dent at his temple line. "I threw her out," he
said in his natural voice. "I couldn't stand it. It was
like training up a dog. That was it. It was like
training up a dog."

Up the hill, on the crest of it, the very tips of the
trees were barely but persistently moving, exchang-
ing the continuous secret of green. He gave it a look,
then walked over to his friend sitting on the ground
there, and put the old hand on the shoulder, as
always, as if the figure on the ground was the one to
be consoled. He always had to do it that way, always. "There was nothing else to her . . . except

what one could see," he said, as he sat down on his stone again. "Nor maybe, I sometimes think it . . . to me."

"All of us," said his friend, getting up from the ground. "Nor to all of us." He picked up his coat, stiffly put it on, and sat down on his own stone. He was silent on his own part for a while.

"Lots of these get-togethers, people ask a widower to," he said then. "Somebody will always bring out a picture of her to show me. Nine times out of ten it'll be one of the ones taken that day. Either from somebody's Brownie, or that long official one with all of us at the windows, or lined up at the start. And when they hear I never got one, they say, "Jim, don't you want one? Here, I can spare it. Here, take this." And maybe they can spare it, maybe nothing came of that day for them. *But, so can I spare it.* And I always tell 'em so. 'I have my own picture right handy,' I always say. 'And what's more, my picture has a back to it, and a smell. I can see the in*side* of the car, and Jim and Emily; that's me and Emily, bending over the cookpot.' And they say, looking sorry for me among one another, 'Oh no, Jim, the cookpot was never inside there; that was back in the hall.' But I say no, that's the way I remember it — or prefer to. 'I remember it all,' I say, 'better than a movie even, better than a Brownie by far.' And then maybe because I feel sorry for them too and they only mean to be nice, I always give them a little laugh. Or maybe because I can't stand for the town to think me a fool. 'Oh,' I say, 'I never have any trouble at all now, keeping those Pardee girls in mind.'"

He fell silent from where he sat now, it was an easy reach to put his hand on his friend's knee. The two old men stayed that way. From the hillside, with what human cargo locked away inside for all anybody knew, from the treetops, deserted in all their glory but not knowing it, from the Little Otselica, no sound came. And then they heard it.

What are these whippoorwill starts in the night, in the bypasses of the night — or is it day? Is this Sand Spring nineteen-twenty, or Sand Spring eighteen-ninety-eight?

It is the ride, banging through the countryside. I can see the long car, the lone car riding its dazzle of rail, and all our heads popping out of the chowder, all our heads at the windows at one time or another, riding the wine-dark night. There are stations, there are stops, and once an owl-call. Then — the solemn forever. Fa-la. Fal-la-la. La, *La.*

The two men listened to it fade. It wasn't dark going back now; it was marvelously clear.

Then the two men got up, with one accord, and looked about them. Had this clearing been kept for them? Was the quiet scene before them awful or serene: Or was it only cheap land for progress, beautiful and stubborn? Each felt he ought to say something about it, but came back to his own life — and halted before speech, even here. One of the two had been marked very early by outer events, but the other even earlier by inner ones. One had left his place of birth but had never doubted his place in the world — and had found it; one had come back to the place where he belonged and had lived his life there — full of doubts. Warriors, returned from wars, and hearing such annals as this afternoon's, could no doubt fall upon one another's shoulders, lean in one another's arms, and heave there; even in modern times, it has been known.

Each for a fact hesitated. But as at every point in their lives when this might have come about — they had been friends too long. Each looked at his friend, his friend standing there in his defenseless prime, and saw how each had come to have the other's facets as well as his own, and why so many of the human race were rightly named — Jim. And this was enough.

Then each walked the other back to the car.

And there, not surprisingly, what with the motor running for the heater to warm them, above which good and faithful sound the voice could slur or sharpen into the practical — it became easy to talk again.

"Housekeepers!" snorted the mate, not moving to go yet. "Jim — will you listen a minute?"

And Jim listened willingly now.

"I know you won't come back to live with me. And though I know I asked you, one time, I don't know now that I really want us to."

"Oh — ?" said Jim, who couldn't keep back a disappointed look, as if now, he'd been about to say yes.

"Because I've got a better idea." The mate warmed the small of his back against the seat, but at the same time thrust forward his forelock, so that all the tendons of chin and neck tightened; maybe he was used to doing this in front of women. The effect wasn't bad. Then he looked Jim over — whom bereavement had thinned, taking away his potbelly. The mate nodded, satisfied. "We're going round the world," he said.

Over Jim's howl of laughter, he talked only the faster, retiring them from business, property and family obligations in a dozen sentences. "The day after the dedication," he said. "The unveiling. That's as good a time as any to tell them. We can leave the day after. The day after, we can start out."

"But I've *seen* the world," Jim murmured. "At least a good part of it. Right here. And you've *been* round it. You flash that card the airlines gave you, often enough."

"Oh, we'll *stop* places," said the mate. "Six months at a time, if we feel like. But you have to give people at home a solid explanation they can hand to others. 'Going around the world, those two,' they can say

[245]

then, and everybody understands it. Have to do that, when you're leaving *permanently*."

Then Jim sat up as if he'd been struck, saying "*Ah*." After a while, he said slowly "But we're not eighty yet. Nowhere near it. I wasn't born till ninety-three." But he couldn't keep a little smile from playing round his mouth.

It was the mate's turn to murmur. "People do it younger these days. This is modern times."

They were both smiling like idiots now, talking out of the sides of their mouths, like old lags. The mate opened the window, and bellowed to the whole audience, of which there wasn't a cow or human — "What are we waiting for!" And Jim answered, "Nothing, just start the car!" but when the mate had done that, his passenger broke into another laughing fit, from which he cried out, "*What* a folly, Jim! They'll never have seen a folly like this one!"

Who was meant by "they" was not spoken of unnecessarily, but you may need to know for later, to keep it by you. It was the "they" to which all such follies are addressed. So, that afternoon theirs was decided upon — or forty years before.

At first, though the car started up all right, the wheels wouldn't catch, having sunk, during the men's meditation, deep into grassy mud. But the two of them were a sturdy pair yet, canny with machines too, still with the strength to push and shove, and the sense where to wedge a stone under a rear tire —

and at last they were free of the treacherous mud of
cheap land, had shaken the dust of the old Batavia
road from their spokes, and were rolling again on the
highway. The pure, long hood of the Cadillac
pointed like a prow, freed of rainbows, and they saw
the weather once more.

Old men, old men. And young.

And so — *said my grandfathers* — we're going
round the world.

We won't ask you to forgive us old men for
taking up your time and trouble. The last thing you
want to do is forgive us — and we know why. It's
because we're what you're going to be. How could
you forgive us for that? But we had to tell you. We
made our miniature, and we had to show it.

So you're going to another war, said my grandfather, and you there are going to fly a plane in it.
The girls among you can only listen of course, but
maybe they can go along for the ride. They're ci-
vilians.

So, listen for *us*, said my grandfather, while we go
around the world. Such odes as we make for the
dead, any of us, are really for the confederation of
the living — for all those who cannot even remember
their own spilt blood, once it has dried; all their
lives, men returned from the wars have plunged for
charm. We are buddies all.

They speak in their sitting room voices, first one,

then the other — our grandfathers — but already as if a clap of thunder has helped them disappear over the horizon.

Who speaks in his own voice, asks my grandfather? And my grandfather answers for him, to him and us. Not we. Not you.

It's all transport, said my grandfathers. In the first things are the last things; this is the roll of the wheel. Wheel and sail, horse and wing, we are going round — fa la la — the world.

How long is it by bicycle to Maple Avenue? See my dust.

See my dust. See my dust. See my dust.

Even from the air, said my grandfathers, faded and gone now.

Even from the air — you won't learn more.

FINIS